"WHY ARE YOU SO AFRAID OF ME?" CULLER asked, watching as she struggled with the question.

"I'm not afraid of you," Pat finally said. "I'm afraid of what you make me feel."

Sighing with heartfelt relief, he pulled her into his arms, then rested his cheek against her hair. "What do I make you feel that's so terrible?"

"Things," she mumbled into his collar.

"But aren't they good things?" he asked, running his hands over her arms.

"I don't know, I just know I don't have time for them. Oh, Culler, there are lots of women who'd jump at the chance to —"

"I don't want lots of women," he murmured, tipping her chin up. "I want you. . . ."

WHAT ARE *LOVESWEPT* ROMANCES?

They are stories of true romance and touching emotion. We believe those two very important ingredients are constants in our highly sensual and very believable stories in the LOVESWEPT *line. Our goal is to give you, the reader, stories of consistently high quality that may sometimes make you laugh, sometimes make you cry, but are always fresh and creative and contain many delightful surprises within their pages.*

Most romance fans read an enormous number of books. Those they truly love, they keep. Others may be traded with friends and soon forgotten. We hope that each LOVESWEPT *romance will be a treasure—a "keeper." We will always try to publish*

LOVE STORIES YOU'LL NEVER FORGET
BY AUTHORS YOU'LL ALWAYS REMEMBER

The Editors

®
658

THE LADY CASTS HER LURES

JACKI REESER

BANTAM BOOKS
NEW YORK · TORONTO · LONDON · SYDNEY · AUCKLAND

THE LADY CASTS HER LURES
A Bantam Book / December 1993

*If you would be interested in receiving protective vinyl covers for your
Loveswept books, please write to this address for information:*

Loveswept
Bantam Books
P.O. Box 985
Hicksville, NY 11802

ISBN 0-553-44413-1

Published simultaneously in the United States and Canada

Bantam Books are published by Bantam Books, a division of Bantam Doubleday Dell Publishing Group, Inc. Its trademark, consisting of the words
"Bantam Books" and the portrayal of a rooster, is Registered in U.S. Patent
and Trademark Office and in other countries. Marca Registrada. Bantam
Books, 1540 Broadway, New York, New York 10036.

PRINTED IN THE UNITED STATES OF AMERICA

OPM   0 9 8 7 6 5 4 3 2 1

For Terry, who makes all
my romantic dreams come true

ONE

Brian Culler shook his head. He didn't want to be at this little social gathering in the hotel ballroom; he wanted to be in his room poring over his well-worn map of Lake Eufaula, concentrating on his strategy for putting the winning catch of largemouth bass in his boat bright and early tomorrow. After placing third in his last two tourneys, he needed this win to put him back at the top of the regional standings. And depositing the big, fat first-prize check for thirty thousand dollars in his bank account wouldn't exactly hurt his feelings either.

While he slugged down cola, Brian once again let his gaze play over the brightly lighted room. He paid no attention to the trade booths lining the walls. He was looking for the writer he was going to be stuck with in the morning—Pat Langston.

She had to be a novice at covering outdoor events because he'd never heard of her, never seen an article or a column with her byline. Just his luck to draw a rank amateur.

He recognized most of the women; some were wives of competitors, some were employees of tackle-and-equipment companies. There were only two he didn't know. One was a pert little blonde working the Top Twine booth and the other was a good-looking brunette clinging to the arm of one of Brian's biggest challengers, Bo Simpson. Standing six-four and weighing two-forty, Simpson was everybody's biggest challenger, Brian thought, amused.

The attractive woman with Bo seemed to have a nice figure, although it was a little hard to tell because of the big blousy black top she wore over hot-pink pants. Brian smiled. Her outfit reminded him of one of his favorite fishing lures, a Firetailed Jelly Worm.

For a moment envy pulled at him. No way would Pat Langston look anything like that attractive number cuddled up to Bo. Grimacing in frustration, he turned his attention to the doorway, waiting for a female in grungy overalls to wedge her way through it and come directly to his side.

While she laughed at the incredibly bad joke Bo Simpson had just told, Pat Langston tightened her arm around him. It had been a couple of weeks since she'd last seen her friend, and she was enjoying the repartee between him and his buddies, although most of the jokes were being told at her expense. The teasing warnings had started as soon as Bo introduced her to Lance Upton and Don Carlisle.

"You did bring a steel chastity belt, didn't you, Pat?" Lance asked her now, a broad grin splitting his tanned face while his amber eyes assessed Pat in a friendly way.

"She won't need a chastity belt. Brian Culler never thinks about sex when he's fishing," Bo countered. "He's all business out on the lake. He's got a six-pound lead. That's sure proof when the fishing's as tough as it was today." Shaking his head, he laughed humorlessly. "Sometimes I think that man *is* a fish."

Pat half listened while she studied the man they were discussing.

Brian Culler looked older than the man who stared out from his press photos. Those black-and-white photos, taken after he'd won the National Championship last year, showed a dark-haired, dark-eyed, square-jawed man who didn't have a care in the world. They didn't show the silver that speckled the dark hair at his temples or the intensity shining from those ebony eyes. They also didn't show the way his new-looking denims gloved his hips and thighs or the way his knit polo shirt fit snugly across his broad shoulders. And no photos could accurately portray the tension created by putting it all on the line and going for the big money in what many considered the craziest professional sport of all, bass fishing.

Pat decided she wouldn't class Brian Culler as "handsome." Too many hours in the sun had given his lean face a weather-beaten quality, making it more rugged than sensual. But she found the sharp creases around his mouth and the straightforward line of his jaw appealing. It was a good face— strong and honest. It might even be a dangerously attractive face if it weren't scowling under the influence of a dark mood.

She'd watch Brian frown as he hastily scanned the room a few times. Only once had she seen him smile, and that had been when another competitor had taken a playful poke at him. As soon as the other man walked away, thunderclouds again descended on Brian's face. Even from this distance she could feel the tension emanating from him, could almost hear the air crackling around him. Grinning, Pat acknowledged she might be imagining the electricity zapping across the thirty feet separating her from Brian. She knew he was waiting—no, *gunning* was a better word—for her.

It didn't bother her to know she was the reason for the man's bad mood. Bo was still embellishing the less-than-encouraging remarks Brian had made after learning she'd be his observer for the final day of this tournament. She doubted the champ knew any more about bass fishing than she did, but she was willing to let him find that out for himself. The major reason she avoided the tournament trail was because of her connection to a former national champ, P. J. McKinley—she avoided falling under her father's shadow as best she could.

Brian wouldn't cast nearly as big a shadow as P.J. According to his bio, the current champ was a native of Chattanooga, Tennessee, and thirty-seven years old. According to Bo, the man she would share a boat with tomorrow was a confirmed bachelor and quite a lady's man when he wanted to be. She wasn't sure if the last piece of information had been meant as a prelude to matchmaking on Bo's part—he'd been known to play Cupid on occasion—or as a warning to be wary of the alluring magnetism of his tournament competitor. Poor Bo. He had no idea how many Brian Cullers she'd run into in her writing career. If they'd ever held any appeal for her, it had long ago been trampled underfoot, along with quite a few of their egos.

Bo also didn't know the extent of her determination to avoid being the lesser half of a male-female relationship. She figured she'd already paid her dues. She'd spent twenty years of her life as "P. J. McKinley's little girl" and ten years as "Michael Langston's little wife."

Her involuntary shudder drew a sharp look from Bo, but she shrugged off his unspoken question, grateful he was too involved in a tall tale to focus fully on her. As he launched into the punch line of his story, she allowed herself a moment of pride in her accomplishments over the past few years. It hadn't been easy, but now she was just plain old Pat Langston, her own person with her own identity. And she wasn't about to give that up for love or money—not that anyone was offering her either at the moment. She had things to do, places to go, goals to achieve, and none of them was compatible with a full-time romance.

Brian Culler was probably one of those good old boys who would never accept her presence in the male-dominated world of this outdoor sport, but he would have to accept her presence in his boat tomorrow. Beyond that she didn't really care what he said or did, or what he thought of her. She had come to Eufaula, Alabama, to do an assignment for a magazine, a feature on a hotshot bass fisherman.

Her old friend Judd Braxton, bless him, had provided the hotshot. It was up to her to provide the feature.

I've fried bigger fish than you, Mr. Brian Culler, she silently promised her subject. Despite his prejudice against her, her story would increase his value to the bass-fishing industry. The thought brought a smile to her lips.

Brian slid his gaze over the brunette, shock jolting through him when he realized she was looking at him with a curious smile on her face. When he smiled and nodded his recognition of her appraising look, she nodded back. It was a slow down-and-up movement of her head, the quirky smile remaining unchanged. There was a surreptitious intimacy in her look, giving him the impression the two of them shared some kind of secret.

Sensing movement in the doorway, he broke eye contact with the woman. He wasn't sure whether he was relieved or disappointed when he recognized each member of the knot of people entering the room. No Pat Langston there. Maybe she wasn't going to show.

In the next instant he looked back at the brunette standing with Simpson, seeing her laugh up into the big man's face. Her loosely curled dark brown hair flowed over her shoulders, catching the light as it shifted with each subtle movement she made. It looked soft and . . . crushable.

Crushable? Brian stifled a groan. *This is no time to think of such things, boy. The only female you need to think about is a bucketmouth sow, a "Momma" largemouth bass.* But despite what his disciplined mind told him, his rebellious feet carried him toward Simpson's little group.

"Hey, Bo," Brian said heartily, "tough break today." Sticking out his hand, he frowned in commiseration. He'd known Simpson for three years, had fished against him in tournaments all across the country. Friendly and affable by nature, Bo was a popular competitor. *Popular with the ladies, too,* Brian conceded, looking at the woman plastered to Simpson's left side. Absentmindedly he shook hands and passed bland comments with Upton and Carlisle, then waited for an introduction to the brunette.

"Yeah, having my motor blow up really cut into my fishing time today," Bo agreed. "It took me three hours to get back to the weigh-in. Those little electric kickers aren't built for speed, Bubba." Simpson called everyone "Bubba," everyone he liked at least. "I'll catch you tomorrow, though, so you'd best keep looking over your shoulder."

"They got you a boat?" Brian asked.

"Yeah, Judd borrowed one from a local." Bo dipped his head, waggling his eyebrows and looking at Pat.

Recognizing the game he was playing, she beamed at him, hoping her heart wouldn't jump clear out of her throat while Brian studied her. Even though she wasn't looking at him, she could feel his dark gaze caressing her with a warmth that was sensually disturbing. With great effort she forced herself to listen to the casual comments the others were making about her friend's fishing skill.

Everyone in that little cluster knew Simpson would never overcome Brian's lead. Bo had amazed them all by bringing in two fish today. Tomorrow he'd be at a distinct disadvantage, fishing from an unfamiliar, creepingly slow boat. While all the other competitors would eat up the lake with their 150-horsepower motors, Bo would be forced to fish close to the weigh-in site because his had only a 60-horsepower motor.

"Hey, Bubba," Bo said suddenly, looking at Brian. "I haven't congratulated you on your day. You made a helluva showing, didn't you? If I weren't fishing tomorrow, I'd think nobody could bump you from first place."

Brian laughed, accepting the backhanded compliment while the brunette's throaty chuckle floated over him like morning sunshine. He dismissed the urge to ask the woman her name as being too obvious and possibly offensive to Simpson. "We all know I've got my work cut out for me tomorrow, don't we? Any of you ever meet this *Pat Langston*? Seen her at any of the tournaments?"

Lance developed a sudden interest in his shoes, and Don cast a nonchalant glance around the room.

A chuckle rumbled from deep inside Bo's chest as he considered the question. "Seems like I met her, years ago." Bo grimaced. "She was . . . you know, the usual."

When Bo's fingers dug into Pat's ribs, warning her to keep quiet, she covered her wince with a smile. Knowing Brian was unjustly prejudiced against her, she would let Bo have his fun. She wished the tournament leader would find somewhere else to focus his eyes, though. Her pulse bounced erratically under the influence of his blatant appraisal of her, and she felt a powerful urge to touch her nose, to see if it was growing longer with each passing second.

"What's 'the usual'?" Brian spoke to Bo, but he continued to look at the woman.

She couldn't be considered beautiful, but there was something about her, an impish kind of devilment, a spirited liveliness he'd bet would be erotically exciting. Checking again the quirky little uplifting of her lips, he decided she had a look of perpetual laughter, as if she found life wonderfully amusing. Even, now, while she was leaning against Simpson, her eyes twinkled with some private joke.

They were nice eyes, Brian decided. Their soft green color invited a man to wade right in and explore the mischief behind them. Noting the little lines radiating from them, he figured she was in her mid-thirties, probably about Bo's age. He had to give his competitor credit, the man knew how to pick 'em.

Simpson's voice demanded Brian's attention.

"Well, let's just say Pat Langston's not what you'd expect." Bo grinned down at the woman at his side. "You know Pat, don't you, *sugar*?" When she nodded, he grinned again. "Well, whatcha think of her?"

"I kind of like her," she crooned, pulling her lips into a coy little pout as she returned Bo's dreamy look. "She's . . . a lot of fun."

Brian stifled a groan. That was all he needed, "a lot of fun" dancing on his concentration tomorrow. Granted, there was a place for "fun," but his boat wasn't it.

"If you see the Langston woman, let me know," he requested, pivoting away from the syrupy looks the brunette was giving Bo. But seconds later, when he heard the booming guffaw that signified something had tickled Bo Simpson's funny bone, envy shot through Brian again. Despite his boasts, Simpson knew he would finish near the bottom tomorrow, so the big man could afford to relax and joke around. He could even afford to switch his concentration from fat-bellied fish with "lockjaw" to long-legged women with gorgeous green eyes.

Feeling more frustrated than ever, Brian cursed his fate again. Would the Langston woman never get here? He was tired, and five a.m. would come too soon. He once more took up his vigil, leaning against the wall across from the door.

"Ouch!" Pretending to be hurt, Bo massaged the spot where Pat's knuckle-fisted blow had landed on his bicep. "Whatcha do that for, *sugar*?" With a quickness belying his size, he sidestepped her next intended blow.

"Enough is enough!" Pat's threatening tone slipped through gritted teeth, but she knew her act wasn't fooling the man she'd known since her toddler days. "It's all right for *you* to try to make a fool of the man, but *I'm* the one who has to spend tomorrow with him. *I'm* the one who'll pay for your little fun and games."

"Aww, no," Bo assured her, his cherubic face suddenly serious. "Brian's really a good guy, *a lot of fun* when the heat's off." Chuckling, he dodged another blow. "He's just a little uptight tonight." He looked at his friends for support of his statement. They both nodded, but neither seemed confident in the assessment.

"*Brian's* uptight?" Pat exclaimed. "You think *Brian's* uptight? How soon they forget." This last was addressed to the ceiling. When she again leveled her gaze on Bo, she was glad to see he had the grace to look sheepish.

"I have seen *you*"—she poked a finger against his broad chest—"when you were within twenty-four hours of winning thirty thousand dollars. Compared with the way you were then, Bo Simpson, Brian Culler's so laid-back, he's practically horizontal!" Pat couldn't explain her sudden urge to defend Brian, but she felt absurdly satisfied about putting her big buddy in his place.

While Bo assured his friends Pat didn't know what she was talking about, she let her gaze wander to the tournament leader. Although Brian was staring at the entry to the room, she had a feeling he wasn't really seeing it. He massaged the muscles in the back of his neck.

"He's figured it out, I tell you." Lance Upton jerked his head toward Brian. "See the way he glances over here at Pat every few seconds?"

Pat followed the direction of Lance's worried frown, feeling her hostile defenses dissolve when the tournament leader grimaced and rubbed the back of his neck. He really looked tired. While she watched, Brian became aware he'd started to stare at her again. He lifted his shoulders in a tiny, apologetic shrug before lowering his hand to his pocket and shifting his line of sight back to the doorway.

She didn't think he'd "figured it out." If he had, he'd have been in her face by now, perhaps rightfully so. Despite the unfairness of Brian's prejudice against her, her heart went out to him when she considered the pressure he must be feeling at the moment.

Thirty thousand dollars was a lot of money, more than she'd made this whole year. To put it simply, Brian Culler was only a few thousand casts away from taking home enough bacon to feed her household for a very long time indeed. Watching as Brian closed his eyes and rested his head against the wall, she decided it was time to let him off the hook.

"I think I should call it a night," she said, smiling up at Bo. "We all have to be up early."

"Yeah, you're right," he agreed, glancing at his watch. "Want me to introduce you to Brian, smooth things over?"

Shaking her head, Pat let her eyes warn him about trying to take care of her. "I'm a big girl now, remember?" She stretched up on her toes and kissed his cheek. "I love you, big fella."

Oblivious to the embarrassment on his friends' faces, Bo caught her hands in his big mitts and smiled down at her. "Love you, too, pretty lady. If Brian gives you any trouble tomorrow, any at all, you let me know. I can still rearrange faces, you know."

Pat nodded. There was no point in arguing. Bo had been her unwanted bodyguard on many occasions. He'd even suffered a bloody nose for her in the second grade.

"Good luck tomorrow, to all of you," she said, shaking hands once more with Don and Lance. All three men were laughing when they strolled away from her.

Now, she thought, *to beard the lion in his den*. Drawing in a deep breath for courage, she took a step, then stopped. *Where was he going?*

Brian was making a beeline for the Top Twine booth. He needed to catch Braxton before the tournament director slipped away with the blonde he'd been hovering over most of the evening. Since the Langston woman hadn't shown up, Braxton had to assign Brian another observer, an unbiased passenger who would make certain he obeyed all the tournament rules. Dragging a hand through his hair as he walked, he smiled with a sudden lighthearted delight. Maybe this time he'd be assigned someone reasonably knowledgeable about professional bass fishing. Someone who'd know to keep his mouth shut.

"Ahh, the man of the hour," Braxton said, holding out his hand. "Gonna be hard for anyone to take this one away from you."

"Now, Judd," Brian countered, "you and I both know it ain't over till the last fish hits the scales." He paused while Judd chuckled over that. "Now, about Pat Langston."

"I knew you'd come around. She's not what you expected, is she?"

Casting a look at the young woman by Braxton's side, Brian tilted his head to one side. "Excuse me?"

"Pat Langston. You two are going to get along just fine, aren't you?"

Brian raised his eyebrows. "I wouldn't know. You got another observer for me in case she doesn't show?"

Braxton opened his mouth, then closed it. His thick brows drew together as he continued to look at Brian a second longer.

"She's right over there," he finally said in puzzled tones, his gray gaze sliding to Bo's brunette, now standing alone on the other side of the room. "I could've sworn you were talking to her a little while ago."

Brian stared at the brunette, his cheeks growing hot as he recalled thinking she'd seemed interested in him. *She was interested, all right. Interested in making a fool of you.*

Wondering how many other people knew Pat Langston had made a total ass of him, he scanned the room looking for Simpson, but that hulk was nowhere to be seen.

Looking again at "Sugar," Brian frowned. She was strolling toward him, that quirky little grin on her face once more. His scowl didn't appear to faze her as she came steadily on, swaying her nicely curved hips just a little more saucily than he thought was necessary.

TWO

"Brian Culler?" Pat stuck out her hand. "I'm Pat Langston." She'd spoken in her most professional voice and she kept her most professional smile in place while she waited for his reaction. The rage behind his flinty stare was palpable.

As his silence continued, she kept her hand out, aware of Judd Braxton's scrutiny. She knew Judd would have introduced her to the other man if she'd given him time, but she'd wanted to assert her ability to stand on her own two feet from the outset.

Braxton put a hand on the other man's arm. "Brian?"

Brian blinked hard, as if awakening from a dream, then tightened his lips into a thin line and nodded. Grasping Pat's hand, he nodded again.

"Yeah, I'm Brian Culler. I've been waiting all evening to meet you, *sugar*."

She hadn't been sure what to expect—whether he would try to prove his superior male strength with a bone-crushing handshake or if he would shrug off the earlier deception. His calloused palm felt warm and firm against her skin, and his fingers enclosed hers with tingling effect, but his acidic tone on the word *sugar* informed her he was not amused by the joke she'd played on him.

Serves you right, Buster, she mentally fired at him, telling herself it was antagonism coiling in the pit of her stomach. Seconds later, when Braxton muttered good-bye, she made an appropriate reply without taking her guarded gaze from Brian's face.

She exhaled slowly and pasted another professional smile on her face. "I know you resent my presence here. But I assure you I won't interfere—"

"You're damned right you won't," he cut in, his voice low but betraying some of the anger he felt. "But just for the record, I don't resent your presence here. I resent your presence in my boat tomorrow. I don't have time to baby-sit some lame-brained neophyte writer who doesn't have the foggiest notion what's at stake." Snaking his hands to his waist, he tipped his head back, eyeing her coldly.

The arrogance in his stance irritated Pat almost as much as his words.

"What's at stake is thirty thousand dollars and a climb in your national ranking, which is already pretty damned good at the moment." Her tone was a mixture of tight control and deadly venom, even though she'd paid him a compliment. "For the record, I've fished with the best, *Mr. Culler.*" After rattling off three of the best-known names in the fishing world, she sucked in a heated breath and rushed on. "I'm here for a story, and," she paused for effect, "you'd better believe I will get my story, with or without your cooperation."

Glaring at him, she told herself she didn't want to go to jail and that's where she'd end up if she gave in to the primal urges she felt toward him at the moment. Her fingers itched to slap that grin off his face. Conscious of the stares of the few people remaining in the room, she fought to maintain her control.

Still stewing over the trick she'd played on him, Brian maintained his stance for several long, silent seconds, smiling his best "Now, calm down, honey," smile. It usually worked with the women in his life on those rare occasions when he was in the doghouse. She wasn't buying his "charmer" look. He might as well try the direct approach.

"Don't take this personally, Ms. Langston," he offered in clipped tones, "but it would be better if we scheduled an interview for after the weigh-in tomorrow. I don't know how much you know about professional bass fishing, but it's my job and I can't do it if you're babbling at me all day."

When she narrowed her eyes on the word *babbling*, he knew he'd struck a nerve, but at that moment he didn't care. He made his living piecing together a puzzle of unknowns: water, wind, weather, structure, depth, and feeding patterns. Having an unknowledgeable writer— someone who'd want to know why he was doing something while he was doing it—added one more unknown. An experienced tournament observer knew enough about fishing to keep quiet, simply to observe and not pass comment or ask questions until the heat was off. Ms. "Sugar Lots-of-Fun" Langston would probably make suggestions as well as ask questions. Or worse, she might want to rummage in his meticulously ordered tackle box. The very thought drew a growl of frustration from him. *Distraction, hell!* Having this woman in his boat was a pro angler's nightmare.

"I'll try not to babble," the source of the nightmare said through barely moving lips. "Just tell me where to be in the morning and what time to be there," she demanded, her sarcastic little smile firing Brian's temper again.

"I'd like to tell you where to—"

"Then tell me that too," she interrupted, slicing a hand through the air. "But do it quickly so I can go to my room. Tomorrow's going to be a long day."

"First, there are some things we need to get straight. While you're in my boat tomorrow—"

"Don't ask for a pit stop, don't speak unless spoken to, don't chew gum loudly or blow bubbles, don't rock the boat—literally. And don't whistle, hum, or sing, either out loud or under my breath. Now, where and when, Mr. Culler?"

He stared at her in slack-jawed surprise, unable to find a comeback. She'd covered all the bases and had even added a few that hadn't occurred to him. She *had* done this before, he realized with a grudging twinge of respect. Feeling as if she'd unfairly stolen all the wind from his sails, he sought a way to recover, a way to get some type of revenge.

Where and when? A few minutes ago, before she'd made a fool of him with her friends, he'd intended to tell her to meet him at five-thirty in the morning. But the fire flashing from those green eyes spurred the devil in him.

The "charmer" smile he flashed this time was guaranteed to melt the Wicked Witch of the West. "Slip Thirty-six, at four-thirty." Noting her upraised eyebrows, he increased the wattage on the grin. "I like to be ready early."

"Slip Thirty-six at four-thirty," she repeated. "I'll be there."

Brian blinked, surprised by the mild response. At a sudden loss for words, he tried the grin again, hoping, for some insane reason, to draw more fire.

Pat wheeled away, only to jerk to a stop when strong, warm fingers curled around her bicep. She spun back to face Brian, her anger flaring again at the sight of the wolfish grin still plastered on his face.

"You haven't *been* with the best, you know," he drawled, accenting the verb when he referred to her earlier comment. "You haven't *been* with me, *sugar*." This time his smile was devastating as his fingers scorched a gentle trail down her arm before he ended the contact.

Shaken by his light caress, Pat felt her anger change to something else, something warm and swirly in her stomach that flowed to her knees with overwhelming speed. Bewildered, she warned herself to be careful. If Brian Culler was suddenly coming over nice and friendly, it probably meant he wanted to make a test run in her bed before they spent the day in his boat.

She let her gaze move downward, her expression remaining cool as she studied the tournament buckle on his belt, the flat abdomen under his zipper, the crisp denim molded over his thighs. Although she was good at hiding her feelings, she had no small problem trying to pretend disinterest in his disgustingly male body. She looked him over again, her eyes moving upward this time until they met his once more. When she opened her mouth to flay him with a withering comment, he cut her off, his words confirming her suspicions.

"Maybe I should walk you to your room." It was a quiet statement, not a request.

Feeling herself on familiar ground, she moistened her lips, softening her expression before she spoke in honeyed tones. "Thanks, but I can manage on my own." Enjoying the moment, she spoke with suggestive innocence. "And if for some reason I should decide not to manage on my own, I'm sure I can find a more suitable escort for my lame-brained neophyte little female self." Smiling with the warmth of a cobra, she made a slow, sedate turn. And found herself crushed against a scrawny chest.

"Cutty!" She squealed the name when she pushed back from the hazel-eyed, white-haired old gentleman who kept his hands on her arms.

"Patsy Jane McKinley!" he returned, his eyes crinkling with interest as they flicked over her face and body. "By God, you look great! I couldn't believe it when Judd said you'd be here. I thought you'd left all us dirty old men way back along the road on your way to fame and fortune." The comment ended with another breath-choking embrace before he once more set her away from him, his gaze going to the man standing behind her.

Brian's amusement over Pat's coy act vanished in confused astonishment when he recognized the man who'd greeted her with such affection. Clive Cuthbertson's picture appeared each month at the head of "Cutty's Catches"— Brian's favorite section in the nation's largest outdoors magazine.

Recovering, he shoved his hand toward the other man. "Brian Culler, sir. I've been a fan of yours for a long time. It's nice to meet you finally after reading your articles all these years." Feeling like a five-year-old talking to Santa Claus, he tried to keep his grin a notch below idiotic when long, bony fingers slid across his palm.

"Please, call me 'Cutty,'" Cuthbertson insisted. "And I'd just as soon not be reminded about 'all these years,' if it's the same to you." Widening the smile, he went on, "Brian Culler, National Champ. Leading the field today, right?"

"Right."

Cuthbertson slid his hand from Brian's grip to Pat's shoulder, pulling her against his short, wiry frame with a familiarity that wasn't lost on the tournament leader.

"Got my girl here in your boat tomorrow, right?"

Wary now, Brian nodded, looking at Pat. He'd earned whatever she dished out now. *You pushed it too far, boy*, he scolded himself. *Now, take it like a man.*

"If I were your competition, I'd protest," Cuthberson said, another wide grin splitting the wizened old face.

"Actually Brian's the one who's protesting," Pat explained. "He objects to my little lame-brained, babbling presence in his boat tomorrow."

"Lame-brained? Babbling? *You?*" Cuthbertson dropped his jaw in exaggerated shock. "You mean he doesn't know—"

"How's Edna, and the boys?" Pat cut in, leaving Brian wondering what it was he didn't know that he somehow felt certain he should know.

Cuthbertson's brow wrinkled in momentary consternation before a smile pulled the corners of his mouth upward. "Edna hasn't divorced me yet. And Frank and Lonnie are doing fine. Didja know I'm gonna be a grandpa?"

"No! You mean one of your boys finally got married? Or did one of them just finally admit to fathering a child?"

Brian watched the interchange with heightened interest, once again seeing the perpetually amused imp in Pat, alias "Sugar," alias "Patsy Jane," Langston. Sadly he realized it was unlikely *he* would ever produce such twinkling little lights in her eyes. The best he could hope for was sparks. He also realized with a sinking heart he'd probably really blown it if she were this well known to a man like Clive Cuthbertson. The old man was a living legend.

"What are you doing here, Cutty? I thought you retired from the tournament scene." Pat looped her arm through the old man's as she spoke.

"I've been working on a special project for the tourney sponsors," he said. "When Judd told me you'd be here, I couldn't resist a chance to visit with you awhile. Let me buy you a drink, and we'll catch up on the last few years." He hesitated, sliding a look to their audience of one. "Unless, of course, you two were—"

"No, we weren't," Pat assured him. "I was just going to my room. Mr. Culler and I have said all we need to say to each other, haven't we?" She beamed a saccharine smile at Brian before continuing. "Besides, our leader here has to be up *very* early tomorrow. I'm sure it's past his bedtime already."

Irritated, Brian considered inviting himself to join them. But realizing he'd already let his temper get him into trouble, he decided to let it go. As much as he'd like to talk with, or better yet listen to, Cutty, he had a nagging feeling it would be wise to take himself off to bed and not ruffle any more of Ms. Pat Langston's feathers.

"Yeah, I gotta be up early," he agreed.

"Good luck tomorrow," Cuthbertson offered. "And no cheating. Remember, Little P.J. is your observer, not your instructor."

For the next several seconds Brian stood in dumbfounded silence, staring after the old man and "Little P.J."

Little P.J.? Patsy Jane McKinley?

By the time this information ricocheted off

the corners of his battered mind, he was torn between abject humiliation and consummate rage.

Pride was a funny thing, Brian mused later, as he waited outside the door to Pat's room. His legs folded up, forearms on knees, he'd been sitting there for nearly half an hour, back against the wall. And that's just how he felt, like his back was against the wall in more than one sense. All because of his stupid pride.

It had been his pride that had prevented him from telling Judd Braxton his reasons for overreacting to Pat Langston's assignment to his boat. Only to himself could Brian admit he was still smarting from his last interview with a writer who knew nothing about fishing.

It had happened after he'd won the National, when one of the Chattanooga papers had asked to do a story. He'd agreed because he'd hoped to publicize the sport of professional fishing and because it would give him a chance to plug his sponsors.

Instead of sending the sports writer Brian expected, the paper assigned a "Lifestyle" reporter who'd nearly driven him nuts with stupid questions. Although he'd managed to remain polite through most of the session, he'd blown a fuse when she told him to strip to the waist for the photo that would accompany the article.

Despite his refusal to pose half naked, the story had read like a Bachelor of the Month feature. To make things worse, the photo had included Brian's house in the background, easily identifiable to anyone familiar with Lake Chickamauga. For weeks afterward women kept "getting lost" in his driveway. If he'd been as hot to trot as the writer had made him out to be, he'd have had enough opportunities for sex to last a lifetime. As it was, he'd been so embarrassed by the tone of the article, he hadn't even sent copies of it to his sponsors.

Yep, he thought again, pride was a funny thing. And in his case it had certainly gone before a fall.

P. J. McKinley. The name kept playing in his mind like a solid-gold cut from a platinum album.

After crawling out of his hand-dug hole of humiliation, he'd paced his room like a caged lion for ten minutes before deciding he had to make his apology tonight. Then, when he'd called Pat's room and gotten no answer, he'd concluded it would be better to let her feed him a generous portion of crow face-to-face. He wasn't going to be able to sleep anyway until he expressed his true remorse to Pat McKinley Langston.

Closing his eyes, Brian tried to focus his thoughts on his strategy for the next day. Head down and lost in his visions of big bass snugged into thick cover, he almost missed Pat's arrival. As it was, she'd stepped past him and opened her door before he realized what was happening.

Without thinking, he wrapped his fingers around her ankle. When he looked up, he wasn't surprised to see her jerk her door shut.

"Why, Mr. Culler, what brings you here at this hour of the night?" she asked in that innocent, little-girl voice she'd used to turn down his offer to walk her to her room.

Brian ducked his head, but he didn't release her ankle. He was trying to figure out how to stand without giving Pat an opportunity to get away. After his rudeness earlier he was certain she would slip into her room and leave him with his apology unspoken if he gave her a chance to do so.

"Why didn't you tell me your father is P. J. McKinley?" he asked, still working on the problem of getting gracefully to his feet. He hadn't realized how hard the cement of the second-level landing was until now. His lean posterior felt as cold and flat as the concrete under it.

"Why should I have told you who my father is?"

"Because." He tilted his head to one side, unable to come up with a good answer to the question.

"Because why, Mr. Culler? Having a great bass angler for a father doesn't make me a great writer, does it?" Weary of him and whatever game he was playing, Pat shook her head in exasperation. "For Pete's sake, will you stand up?"

The look he gave her started out as mildly sheepish and swiftly became profoundly embarrassed. "I'm not sure I can."

"What do you mean, you're not sure you can?" It was taking every bit of willpower she possessed to ignore the heat radiating from his grip on her ankle. It wasn't an unpleasant sensation, just a disturbing one that defied the law of gravity by flowing upward through her stomach to her lungs, somehow restricting her breathing.

"I—" He paused, and attempted a grin. "I've been here a long time, waiting for you. Could you help me up?"

Pat stared at him. When he continued to look at her with the expression of a chastised beagle, her anger melted away. She'd prepared for an argument, had braced herself for another heated harangue from him. Now she found herself totally at a loss as to how to deal with his helplessness.

"Let go of my ankle and I'll help you up." It seemed like a reasonable trade.

"You won't run into your room?"

"What?" Her vexed tone was a fair indication of her incredulous reaction to the childishness of his question.

"If I let go of your ankle, you won't just take off before I can stand up, will you?"

"Brian! Stop this foolishness—*now*," she ordered in the tone of voice she used with her children when they'd pushed her to the edge of her patience.

With an ironic smile Brian uncurled his fingers from her ankle and held up his hand to her.

Pat didn't give herself time to worry about the consequences of taking that hand. Without hesitation she stepped in front of Brian, clutched his fingers, and pulled. Too late she realized he really needed assistance to get to his feet.

Expecting to pull against Pat's steadiness, Brian lurched upward. Too late he realized she hadn't taken his request for assistance seriously. He teetered momentarily on deadened limbs, fighting a losing battle with balance.

As he fell, he jerked his hand from Pat's, hoping she could remain upright. His head struck the wall in the same instant his posterior landed on the cold, hard concrete, but he ignored the sudden pain in the back of his skull. His attention was riveted to Pat. A little shriek slipped from her when she toppled forward, and Brian's eyes widened when he recognized where she would land. *Move!* his instinct for self-preservation shouted at him. But it was too late.

In less than two heartbeats Pat went from standing upright to sprawling between Brian's legs, her nose crinkled against his chest and her knees stinging from the impact with the hard flooring. Breathing hard, the twinges in her knees painful, she took in a scent so essentially male, it shot confusion to every part of her body. Struggling to get up, she stopped wriggling when Brian groaned in complaint.

Trapped between their bodies, her right hand pressed palm downward against his fly. In her attempt to rise she'd inadvertently pushed against that tender portion of his anatomy. As if that weren't dreadful enough, the fingers of her left hand were spread over the inside of his right thigh, dangerously close to his groin.

"You did that on purpose," she accused, raising her head to nail him to the wall with her stare. Incredibly, she felt the bulge under her right palm gain substance in reaction to her movement. "Of all the cheap tricks!"

Brian was looking at her in comic confusion,

his onyx eyes rounded in acknowledgment of the potential danger to his future ability to produce children. "It wasn't a trick, I promise. I really thought you were going to help me. I told you I didn't think I could get up."

"You seem to be doing a fine job of 'getting up,'" Pat snapped, her cheeks growing hot as soon as the words flew from her lips. "Oh, God, how do I get into these situations?" At that moment she sympathized with a fish flopping on shore. Her legs were numb and useless, and her hands were—Better not think about her hands, she decided.

Rolling her weight to the left, she yanked her right hand free, gasping when Brian's legs snapped together in a belated and useless reflex. "Let me go, Brian Culler," she choked out in her most venomous tones.

His muscular grip on her ribs eased, but she could feel the tension rippling through his taut thighs while he studied her from under thick lashes. In that instant she found herself hoping the emotion smoldering in those eyes was anger. She didn't want to know about anything else that could turn onyx into smoke.

"I'm not holding you," Brian insisted, bucking under her as if she were an unwanted rider he could dislodge.

"That's not helping anything." Her cheeks

flamed as his problem grew beneath her. "Be still and let me push off your chest." Grunting against the sudden rush of blood to her knees and the resurgence of tenderness it emphasized, she slid her hands to Brian's ribs and shoved herself upright as if she were pushing off a hot stove.

Despite her annoyance with him, she was unable to contain a smile while she watched his efforts to get to his feet. First he did a slow roll to his knees, pausing for several seconds while he grumbled about the condition of his posterior. Then he pushed himself off the concrete floor and rose from its surface backward, looking like an inchworm unfolding into an upright position.

As soon as he straightened, he began massaging his backside. "You didn't play fair with me, you know," he muttered.

"*I* didn't play fair? *You're* the one who pulled me down!"

"I mean, you didn't play fair when we met. You should have told me you're P. J. McKinley's daughter."

She refused to let him douse her with guilt. "You didn't give me much of a chance to tell you anything, did you?"

He shrugged. "Judd could have said something to me."

"I've fought pretty hard to be my own person,"

she offered in conciliatory tones. "I want people to respect me for my talents and for my skills, not because I'm related to a person they admire. I've worked hard to become somebody other than the great P. J. McKinley's little girl." *Or Michael Langston's little wife*, she thought.

"He is, you know," Brian said, sounding like an awestruck kid. "Great," he added, as if she might not have understood his meaning.

Pat gave a bark of laughter. "Yeah, I know. He *is* great. A legend. 'The father of modern-day structure fishing.' I've known the man for nearly thirty-four years. You don't have to sell me on him."

But her irritation returned when she considered her long battle to be her own person. "If that's why you were camped on my doorstep—so you could harass me for being P. J. McKinley's daughter—consider your mission accomplished. Now, I have a *very* early appointment at Slip Thirty-six. Good night, Mr. Culler."

"That's not why I'm here."

She'd already started to push open the door when his hand descended on hers. At the unexpected contact sensual awareness skittered up her arm, and her neck tingled. But panic didn't penetrate until Pat looked into Brian's dark eyes and saw something that was definitely not anger.

"I wanted to see you," he murmured, "to apologize. I was rude and out of line tonight. I'm sorry."

"Is this apology for Little P. J. or for Pat Langston?"

"For both, I guess."

He stared at her mouth, his husky tones tiptoeing down her spine. Wishing he would look her in the eye, Pat found herself reluctant to speak again, but if she didn't, Brian might continue to occupy her personal space all night.

"Okay, apology accepted," she said, wondering what had happened to her old stiff backbone. At the moment she felt boneless, unable to move. And then she remembered. Brian respected and admired her father, not her. "Tomorrow's going to be a long day."

His failure to take the hint didn't surprise her. She'd already learned he wasn't big on subtleties. Yet when he leaned closer and she inhaled his woodsy cologne and marvelous natural scent, Pat knew she was in danger of losing the professional distance her job demanded. Feeling drugged, she reminded herself of the strong hero worship her father inspired in bass anglers. Brian was merely transferring his esteem for P. J.

McKinley to "Little P. J." It had happened in the past.

"Good night, Brian," she said again, drawing her right knee into a defensive position she'd learned at an early age.

Watching her shapely lips form his name, Brian dazedly decided crow wasn't so distasteful after all. He might even grow to like it, if Pat would talk to him while she fed it to him. When her "good night" finally intruded on his fascination with her lips, he breathed in her fragrance a second longer, enjoying the lightheadedness it caused.

"You don't have to be at the boat until five-thirty." Dragging his gaze from her luscious-looking lips, he focused on her wide eyes. "I was being . . ." His gaze drifted once more to her disturbingly distracting mouth.

"Childish?"

"Yeah, childish," he agreed, nodding his head in an almost imperceptible manner, eyes still glued to her lips. *Get a grip, man! You've got a tournament to win.* Forcing himself to think of thirty thousand dollars, he straightened and tried to sound stern. "I just thought of one more 'don't' "

Pat stiffened. "What's that?"

"Don't wear that perfume tomorrow. It makes my head swim." Determined to ignore the hardness and fire in his loins, he flashed one more charming smile before he turned and ambled away, whistling tunelessly through his teeth.

Stunned by his last, quiet command, Pat sagged against the doorframe, watching him go. She'd never encountered anyone quite like the volatile, dark-eyed Brian Culler. Granted, in her job she always encountered men who came on to her, simply because she was a woman and they felt it their duty to offer her a night or two of passion. Brian, on the other hand, had approached her without words, his aura enfolding her with warm, pleasurable sensations.

Later, as she lay awake in bed with thoughts of him robbing her of sleep, she asked herself if perhaps she should request a change in her boat assignment.

"Don't be ridiculous! You've spent most of your life around men in boats," she said out loud, as if hearing the words would make them more convincing. "Brian Culler is just another story, just another hotshot bass fisherman."

But even now, when she was more asleep than awake, she could recall the fit of Brian's jeans, the strength in his shoulders, the planes of his face. She could still feel the controlled energy that seemed to make the very air move around the man.

Groaning, Pat punched her pillow. Tomorrow was indeed going to be a long day.

THREE

Feeling as if he was slogging through a river of sludge, Brian shuffled from his room into the predawn gray outside. For the first time in all his years of tournament fishing he'd overslept, and it was all Pat Langston's fault. She'd refused to leave his mind, even after he'd ordered her out. Dammit! What had she been doing in his dreams all night long?

A dull throb in his groin reminded him exactly what *she'd* been doing in his dreams. What *he'd* been doing. What *they'd* been doing.

He trotted up to Slip 36, where two people waited. Without stopping, he stepped onto his bass rig and automatically held out his hand to Pat.

"Hey, Bubba, we were just about to send out the cavalry. You okay?" Bo Simpson asked.

"Yeah. I, uh, I was, uh, studying my map and lost track of the time." Looking closely at Pat when she took his hand, Brian felt his heart thud against his ribs.

"Good morning," he managed to say, grateful for the gruff tone that covered the sudden weakness of his voice. Pat might not be wearing that head-spinning perfume, but she looked too damned cute for comfort with her hair pulled up under a baseball cap like a teenager at the local sports arena. The lettering on the bright pink cap brought a smile to his face. It read, FISHERMOM.

"May I keep this bag close by?" she asked as she hopped onto the casting platform, jerking her hand free the instant her feet made contact with the carpeting. "My camera's in here, along with all my other gear."

"Sure." He couldn't contain a wince at the sight of the bright yellow gearbag, but he managed a halfhearted grin. "At least I won't have any trouble seeing it."

"I'll keep it out of your way," she assured him, her expression serious in the predawn light.

Realizing he had ten minutes in which to accomplish what he usually did in thirty, Brian went about his business, grateful for Pat's determination to stay out of his way. Yet in spite of *his* determination to ignore her, he was acutely conscious of the fit of her dark brown jumpsuit, a fit that nearly sucked a whistle from him when she folded onto the seat at his motioned command. Everything her baggy clothes had hidden the night before was neatly packed into that form-fitting jumpsuit. *No distractions*, he reminded himself sternly.

Moments later he backed the boat from its slip and joined the others in front of the marina, glancing at his watch. He'd made it with two minutes to spare before the "ease-off." As he pulled on his goggles, he looked at Pat.

"You got goggles?"

She was unzipping her yellow bag when she answered absentmindedly. "No, I don't."

"Dammit," he grumbled with frustration. "You know you can't ride across this lake at sixty-five miles an hour without goggles!" He fumbled with the catch on the rod box where he kept extra gear. While he rummaged, he noticed Don Carlisle, a few boats away; the man had a wide, amused— and very irritating grin on his face.

The instant his fingers closed over the spare goggles, Brian snatched them free and held them out to Pat while he pushed the throttle forward in response to the signal for the ease-off. When she didn't take them from him, he glanced at her. His involuntary double take allowed him a momentary glimpse of Pat's smile before she flipped down the smoke-colored visor of her hot-pink motorcycle helmet.

Several times during the first few minutes of fishing, Brian clamped down on the urge to ask P. J. McKinley's daughter if she approved of his technique. It was an urge he expected to battle all day, but when he netted his first "keeper" bass only thirty minutes after leaving the marina, he relaxed and forgot about his observer. Almost.

Each time he moved to a new location on the lake, he made one of those "nice day" kind of comments he'd make to someone he met on the street. Each time Pat answered in the same tone and with a similar pleasantry. He had to give her credit, she was certainly the quietest observer he'd ever had in his boat. She didn't utter one word, except in response to a direct comment from him.

For nearly five hours the monotony of the lure sailing out and being rapidly reeled in was broken only when they moved to a new location. Or when Brian's grunt broke the stillness.

When he lowered the fourth fish into his

livewell, excitement scampered through Pat's veins. Brian was having a helluva day, and she was going to get a helluva story. One more "keeper" and the champ could begin culling.

In the big-money game of professional bass fishing, nothing within size restrictions was thrown back until the angler had his limit in the livewell. Competitors were allowed to weigh in a maximum of five live, healthy fish, and they were penalized for bringing dead fish to the scales. Smiling to herself, she recalled some of her father's most famous words: "There's a fine line between men who fish and fisher-men." As befitted the current National Bass Trail Champion, Brian Culler was a fisher-man. A pro.

When he made another cast she raised her camera and studied the nauseatingly photogenic man. She'd assessed a lot of men's buns through the viewfinder, but none in her memory could hold a candle to Brian's. He was probably enrolled in a bun-building course at some exclusive health club restricted to playboy bachelors, she decided. He certainly hadn't gotten that physique from cleaning house and taking care of children.

Trying to picture Brian with a baby on his hip and a toddler wrapped around his knees made her grin. No way could she bring that picture into focus. And if she didn't get her mind on her work, she was never going to get the pictures she needed to accompany her article. She clicked the shutter when Brian flicked his wrist and sent the lure sailing out over the water again.

Oblivious of everything but the feel of the lure swimming through the water, Brian retrieved it before checking the sun's position. In the next instant he set down the rod he'd been using, switched on the trolling motor, and reached for his Flip'N'Stick. It was time to get in there among 'em.

He tingled with anticipation as always when he held the stiff Stick in his hands. He much preferred going one-on-one with big fish to cranking the deep water, but he knew it was going to take both skills to win this tournament.

Scanning the shoreline of the large cove he'd scouted two days earlier, he aimed the boat for the thickest cover in the darkest patch of shade. While the rig slipped silently over the water, he thought about the tanned smoothness of Pat's legs, her sun-darkened skin set off by the near white shorts she was wearing now. Until he'd glanced at her after catching the last fish, he hadn't realized she'd slipped out of the jumpsuit at some point. Unfortunately his attention had been riveted on deep-water structure fishing;

he'd have exchanged a fish in his livewell for the opportunity to watch her squirm out of that close-fitting garment.

"You live in Lincolnton, Pat?" Although his voice was hoarse from lack of use, it sounded overloud in the silence of the day.

Startled, Pat stared at the dark patch of sweat on the back of Brian's long-sleeved shirt. When he repeated the question, she cleared her throat and answered cautiously.

"No. I don't live in Lincolnton." She wasn't surprised he knew her hometown, he was a P. J. McKinley fan, wasn't he?

"Where *do* you live?"

"Atlanta." She started to add "Georgia," but didn't want to sound obnoxious. She wanted to maintain the noncombative atmosphere of the day, if possible.

"Family there?"

"Yes."

Nudging his hat back with his forearm, Brian twisted around to look at her. "A real talker, aren't you?"

"Sometimes."

When his abrupt laughter echoed across the water, Pat withdrew even farther into herself. Before he'd discovered her family heritage, Brian had made it clear he disapproved of her and her career. She eyed the set of his shoulders when he faced front again.

"I take it you're not married?"

"Why do you take it?" she asked.

"No rings."

Automatically Pat tucked her left hand behind her. She didn't know why it bothered her to know he'd noticed the absence of rings there, but it did.

After a few seconds he sighed. "Divorced?"

Although he couldn't see her, she shrugged. "Yes."

"Isn't everybody?"

"You're not."

Brian caught something in her tone that said his single status left him unqualified to discuss divorce. Deciding she was right, he jumped into his next question—one spurred by her God-awful pink hat. "You have children, right?" The boat covered several yards of water before he heard her answer.

"Yes."

Jerking his head around to look at her again, he demanded, "How am I ever going to convince you that I'm really a nice, polite, *charming* fellow if you act like this is an interrogation?"

"Isn't it?"

"No, it isn't." Tamping down the urge to wring her pretty neck, he tugged his cap down low over his eyes.

"Then why are you asking me all these questions?"

"Just being friendly."

Noting the stubborn jut of his chin, Pat shook her head. "Look, you made it clear to me last night, you don't like me and you don't like what I do for a living. I see no point in pretending to be friendly. Today is business, for both of us. Period."

Turning toward the front of the boat again, Brian shoved his hat back and dragged his sleeve over his forehead. "I apologized for last night."

"Only because I'm P. J. McKinley's daughter."

He peered over his shoulder. "You don't know that for a fact. Maybe I was going to apologize before I found out about your father."

"Yeah, and maybe I'll be a *Playboy* centerfold one day."

"Doesn't that chip on your shoulder get a little heavy?"

Undaunted by his thunderous expression, Pat returned the look, unwilling to admit he was right. She was a little sensitive sometimes.

All right, she argued with her conscience, she

was being a lot sensitive right now. It stemmed from her strange feelings about Brian Culler. She knew better than to be attracted to a man who spent all his time on the road and had never committed himself to anyone but himself.

"Men like you have put that chip there for me, Brian. Sorry you don't care for it."

She was grateful when he kept his retort to a disgusted snort and faced forward again, slowing the boat as it approached a partially submerged tree. Apparently oblivious of her once more, he drew in a deep breath and raised the rod, dangling the lure above the jumble of limbs for an instant before lowering it.

Although she'd observed his deep-water tactics without a great deal of interest, Pat now studied every move Brian made. Thanks to her practical education, she knew that bright days like this forced the fish to hide in thick cover like the heavy brush Brian was now probing. Once tucked into a protective spot, the fish rarely moved, even for an easy meal. Instead the bass would lie peacefully in its chosen spot, simply opening its mouth and flaring its gills to suck in the food—"inhaling it," in a manner of speaking. It was a lightning-quick process, and anyone who'd ever watched goldfish knew how promptly they could also spit out, or "exhale," something that didn't taste or feel quite right.

Flippin', the art of silently placing the lure directly in front of the fish, was the angler's answer to the problem. However, very few people had the necessary combination of mental discipline, uncanny intuitiveness, and constant readiness to excel at the tactic. Pat knew that when it came to flippin', Brian Culler was the best of the best, as he'd proven by winning the National Championship with this technique.

Watching his movements, she felt as if she were caught in some kind of Alfred Hitchcock thriller. Each time the feathery-looking lure descended into the water, she expected Brian to set the hook.

Although he appeared to be relaxed, she knew all systems were "go" with him and she doubted a dozen naked women could distract him at the moment. She was certain a dozen naked men couldn't distract her from watching him—unless one of them was Brian Culler himself.

Now where did that come from? Pat fanned her face, telling herself she hadn't seen a naked man in more than four years and there wasn't any point in thinking about one now, even one as nicely built as Brian. Now was the time to concentrate on the man's skill, to memorize his every move so that she could accurately describe his tactics for her readers.

Fifteen minutes later her attentiveness was rewarded with a quick jolt through the boat and the chesty grunt she'd come to associate with a hook-setting Brian. In the manner of a pro, he put everything he had into his hook-set. Considering the intense energy inherent in the man, Pat would bet good money he put everything he had into everything he did.

Of necessity the battle was a short one. The fish was on the business end of less than ten feet of line when Brian hauled it from the brush. When the bass wallowed on top of the water, he scooped the net under it and lifted it into the boat in one motion. Seconds later, with an efficiency born of years of practice, he removed the hook from the mouth of the fat-bellied "hawg" and lowered the fish into his livewell.

"Looks like another 'keeper,'" Pat drawled in a casual understatement. She figured the fish would weigh in at better than eight pounds, making it a strong candidate for the thousand-dollar Big Fish Award.

"Yeah," Brian agreed, turning away so she couldn't see his shaking fingers. "That 'Pretty Woman' has made me a very happy man."

Although he hadn't smoked in more than five

years, at that moment he wanted a cigarette so badly, he could damned near taste it. Making a conscious effort to dispel the craving for nicotine, he sucked in and expelled several deep breaths.

When he returned his attention to the thick brush in front of the boat, a soft chuckle escaped him as he remembered a conversation he'd had with a young competitor, Seth Henderson, who'd compared fishing to sex. According to the kid, when it was good, it was very, very good, and when it was bad, it was still very good. Recalling the rush of pleasure he'd experienced when he'd set the hook on the big bass, Brian conceded the kid just might have something there.

An hour later, after he'd fished every stick-up in the cove and culled the smallest fish from his livewell, he set down his rod and rolled his head in circles. Slowing his movements, he pleasured himself with the sight of Pat's shapely legs, smiling when she tipped her hat back and looked into his eyes. She didn't flinch under the directness of his appraisal. She merely kept her gaze locked with his, challenging him. It took a great deal of effort for Brian to refrain from suggesting they make love right then and there.

Glued to Brian's smoldering gaze, Pat gradually realized there was something different about him at the moment. Although there was a certain amount of tension in the air around him, his now-hatless frame seemed uncharacteristically loose. When he flashed his sexy grin and sauntered toward her, she thought perhaps she'd dozed off and was dreaming.

No, she decided, the man who stopped in front of her was no imaginary conception. She was forced to tilt her head back to meet his dark gaze, but that was preferable to focusing on the view directly in front of her—a view that included his pewter belt buckle.

Uncomfortable with her position and uncertain about Brian's intentions, she quickly got up. Too late she realized how very close he was standing. When her breasts brushed against his shirt, she stepped back, gasping when he pulled her against his chest. Although she glared at him through narrowed eyes, she didn't attempt to move away. Her nipples puckered against the sweat-moistened warmth of his chest, and she wasn't about to let Brian know he was creating, too, a sweet confusion between her thighs.

"What do you think you're doing?" she managed to ask.

"Saving you." His voice was a soft caress up her spine.

Forcing her eyes away from his, Pat examined the raised casting platform inches from her heels.

Brian actually had saved her from a tumble. Afraid to meet his gaze again, she spoke to his chin. "You can let me go. I'm safe now."

"I'm not sure I am."

The quiet statement made her catch her breath. Her eyes moved from his chin to his mouth, and in that moment she realized she wanted him to kiss her. She wanted to find out if Brian's mouth was as alive as the rest of him, if his energy would pour into her. She wanted to know if his lips would read her as easily as his fingers read the structure he fished. Recognizing the danger in what she was thinking, she ordered her brain to come to her assistance in the battle raging within her. It did . . . and at last she found strength to speak.

"You're safe, but your thirty thousand dollars aren't." Her knees wobbled and her breath escaped in slow relief when his head stopped its downward movement and a cocky grin spread over those energetic, sensuous lips.

"You're right," he agreed, releasing her. "About the money, that is," he added, stepping past her to get into the driver's seat.

Four hours later, when he eased the boat into line with the other competitors waiting for the weigh-in, Brian was feeling very, very good.

"Whatcha got, Culler?"

"Twenty-two pounds, give or take a few ounces, all looking good right now," he told the tournament staffer who pulled alongside him. It was a standard question. To build the suspense of the weigh-in, the probable winner was always the last to bring his fish to the scales. But if his fish were suffering from long hours in a livewell, the angler would be moved up in the line.

"Big fish?"

"About eight pounds." He smiled when the younger man whistled his appreciation. "Whatcha think?"

The other man dipped his head, then winked. "Looks good, Culler, *real* good. Seth's the only one not in yet, but he was way behind you yesterday. Most of the guys are grumbling about the weather."

Brian nodded. Fishing was easier under overcast skies. Still smiling, he watched the tournament staffer ease up to another boat, then glanced at Pat.

"Fire away," he said, chuckling when he saw her pen already poised over her notepad.

"I've got most of your personal background from your bio, but is there anything you'd like to add to it?"

"Nope. Most of it's true."

Pat raised an eyebrow at him, wishing he would turn down the smile a notch or two. That blinding flash of white made her feel like a little pig staring into the face of the Big Bad Wolf.

"You started fishing full-time five years ago, right?" When he nodded, she went on. "What made you decide to risk making your entire livelihood from sportfishing?"

She knew her readership included a large number of weekend fishermen who dreamed of fishing for a living. They loved success stories about guys who'd done it and survived. Brian had more than survived, he'd earned nearly two hundred thousand dollars in the past year alone.

"For nearly ten years I was a weekend fisherman like a lot of other guys," he said. "Then I got a lucky break, managed to win a few tourneys, and found a sponsor. Here I am, five years later, still getting lucky breaks now and then."

As she finished scrawling his answer, Pat asked her next question. "A lot of the competitors here are bemoaning the clear skies today, but you seem to like these conditions. Why?" She already knew the answer, but she wanted it in his words.

As he talked, Brian explained how he preferred

the really challenging days, how he spent hours fishing in just this kind of weather. Of course he spent hours fishing in all types of weather. When he wasn't tournament fishing, he was . . . fishing.

"Does it bother you when people don't take your sport seriously?"

Considering his answer, Brian stood once more, moving to check the fish in his livewell. He was restless now, ready to collect his money and relax. Casting a glance toward Seth Henderson's rig, he allowed himself one derogatory thought about "luck."

"Yeah, it bothers me sometimes," he admitted. "No one thinks it strange if a professional athlete whose specialty is, say, football or tennis, spends most of his time practicing his sport. But because I practice in a boat, on a lake, there are people who think I'm not working."

"It's difficult when people don't respect what you do for a living," Pat interjected into the silence that followed his statement.

He fixed her with a sheepish stare. "Yeah, it is. I guess you know about that, don't you?"

She nodded. "I ran into a little trouble with that just recently."

Brian walked back to her. "I really am sorry about last night. My mouth was disconnected from my brain for a while." Easing down into his seat again, he gave her an embarrassed little smile. "I'd like to buy you dinner this evening, to make up for my bad behavior last night."

Pat's eyes widened in what he took to be disbelief. "You don't have to do that," she protested.

"In that case I'd like to have dinner with you, period."

"Thanks, but I'm having dinner with Bo." She hesitated before rushing on, "Why don't you join us?"

"No, thanks. Three's a crowd." Wincing, Brian remembered that he'd almost kissed her earlier. *You know better than to make a move on a friend's woman*, he scolded himself.

After that he contented himself with watching the other boats leave, but in spite of her silence he was keenly aware of Pat's presence. His left thigh, only inches from hers, felt as though it might burst into flames, and his left hand begged to leave the steering wheel. By the time a tournament staffer gestured Brian to the boat ramp, his muscles were twitching in rebellion. Moments later, when he helped Pat step from the boat, he hoped she'd chalk up the slight trembling in his fingers to weigh-in jitters.

Eyeing the jumpsuit once more in place over her shorts and T-shirt, he admitted to himself she'd surprised him, in more ways than one. Her silence had been admirable all day; in the ten hours they'd been on the lake, she hadn't complained and hadn't asked stupid questions. She hadn't even pestered him about photos, although he might have been willing to strip to the waist, or further, if she'd asked.

Cut it out, he ordered his overactive libido as he placed his bag of fish on the scales. Concentrating on erasing Pat Langston from his awareness, he failed to catch the significance of the crowd noise. When he realized Judd Braxton was talking to him, Brian looked at the leader board. He'd won the tournament and the Big Fish Award.

While Braxton made the official announcement, Brian ducked his head in genuine embarrassment. He didn't like this part of professional fishing. He'd be happier if he could weigh in his fish and leave, getting the check through the mail.

"Brian, it's been your tournament from the start," Braxton declared. "Why don't you say a few words to these people?"

Although he hated to make these little speeches, he tried to be gracious in accepting the microphone from Braxton. It was all part of the game, part of the show. Getting people excited about fishing was what brought in the sponsors and fattened the purses.

"I'm grateful for this beautiful weather," he began, grinning at the chorus of groans from the crowd. "And, as always, I'm grateful to my sponsors." He named the three major manufacturers who paid his tourney fees and supplied him with equipment. "I'm also glad I live in the greatest country in the world," he went on, ignoring the tightness in his chest when he saw Pat Langston at Simpson's side. "Only in America, folks, can a man pursue his dreams to the fullest." He knew it sounded corny, but it was true, and he never missed a chance to say it.

"I have some bad news," Braxton pronounced when Brian shoved the microphone at him. "Miss Lake Eufuala is unable to be here, so I guess Brian will have to accept his winnings from me. But he'll have to forgo the usual kiss."

"I've got an idea," Bo Simpson's deep voice rang out. "Pat can give Brian his kiss." He waved away Pat's yelp of protest. "Now, sugar, you told me you got a great story today. Surely you can do us this little old favor."

Arching his eyebrows at Simpson, Brian wondered if the man was crazy. Noting Pat's reddened cheeks, he decided to stop the whole thing before it got out of hand.

"I appreciate the offer," he shouted above the crowd noise. "But I'll just make it up next time. I'll take two kisses at the next tournament, okay, Judd?" As he'd known it would, his assumption that he would win the next tournament brought a clamor from the crowd.

Braxton nodded, but Bo was already moving to the platform steps, dragging Pat along with him. She looked up at Brian with head-shaking resignation, catching his apologetic smile as he copied her negative movement. Feeling like a lamb being led to slaughter, she walked up the steps and strode to the tournament winner.

"Let's get this over with quick, okay?" she whispered.

He whispered too. "May I remove your hat?" When she shrugged, he tugged the cap from her head, smiling when the long, thick ponytail fell onto her back. The crowd "ooohed" at the action, then grew quiet. "How do you want to do this?"

Pat blinked. "I beg your pardon?"

"I mean, do you want to kiss me, or should I kiss you, or should we meet somewhere in the middle?"

She tried to remember if she'd ever talked about a kiss before the fact. Kissing was something you simply did, wasn't it? She looked at Brian in helpless distress.

"Should we count to three?"

"Yes," she said, clutching at the straw he offered. "Then just do whatever it is you usually do." She couldn't believe she was nervous about this. Hadn't she wondered a few short hours ago what it would be like to be kissed by Brian Culler?

"Are you ready?"

She nodded, then realized he was waiting for her to start counting. "One . . . two . . ."

That was as far as she got before he kissed her while burying the fingers of his right hand in the hair at the back of her neck to hold her in place. It wasn't necessary; she wasn't going anywhere.

She'd wanted to know what it would feel like—well, now she knew. It was possibly the most delightful experience of her life.

While her lips responded to the gentle pressure on them, a solid, burning ache climbed her body. And her knees . . . well, they weren't even present and accounted for, they'd abandoned ship. Moaning softly, she leaned into Brian's chest, giving herself up to the magic whirling through her.

"Hey, Judd! Looks like Brian doesn't want the money!"

Seth Henderson's voice cut through the haze in Brian's brain, forcing him to break the delicious contact. Drawing in shallow breaths, he steadied Pat while he waited for her to open her eyes.

"Maybe I *will* join you and Bo for dinner, after all," he said when she blinked at him in confusion.

FOUR

Curling her fingers into fists, Pat glared at Bo Simpson when he tossed her a little salute from the doorway as he left the restaurant that evening.

"Too bad about Bo's motor." Brian's comment only cut through Pat's red haze; it drew no sympathy from her. "It's hard to keep your gear in shape when you're not finishing in the money," he went on, obviously trying to encourage her to talk.

Still fighting her anger, Pat picked up her menu and glared at it. She didn't for a moment believe Bo had to meet with the mechanic who was going to work on his boat motor. No mechanic worked this late on a Friday evening.

"Pat? Are you okay?" There was genuine concern in Brian's voice now.

Blinking, she shook her head, then nodded, flustered by Bo's circumvention of her first rule of survival: Never put yourself in a compromising situation. It was during her first outdoor writers' conference that she'd learned how quickly a friendly, outgoing woman could find herself fending off unwanted advances. That time she'd agreed to have dinner with a writer whose work she'd long admired. She'd still worn a wedding ring then and hadn't been prepared for the after-dinner wrestling match that ended in embarrassment for both her and the man. And she'd been stunned by the writer's inference that she'd led him on. Since then she'd approached social occasions with a caution she believed was as necessary as it was justified.

"Relax, Pat," Brian urged. "I promise I won't tuck my napkin under my chin or stir my food with my fingers. And I'll try hard not to drool on my tie."

"You're not wearing a tie," she countered, eyeing the dense salt-and-pepper curls exposed in the vee of his aqua polo shirt with the inevitable sponsor logo above the pocket. Pushing back her chair, she attempted a smile. "I'm sorry, Brian. I think I'll just order room service."

"You're never going to forgive me for last night, are you?"

Surprised, she sat open-mouthed for several seconds. "Last night is over and done with," she finally said. "I believe you're really sorry about it."

"Then have dinner with me. You've got to eat sometime, and I promise I'll behave. I won't get out of line."

Swallowing hard, she told herself it was all right. No harm could come from simply eating dinner, especially here, in this busy restaurant. If Brian caused her any reason for worry, she could be in her room in five minutes. Alone.

She scooted her chair back under the table. "I'm sorry about Bo's tactics."

Grinning like a kid at Disney World, Brian pretended shock. "What? You mean Bo planned this?"

"Yes," she assured him, reaching for her glass of water. "He thinks I should date more often."

"Should you?"

Catching a challenge in the question, Pat took three long swallows before lowering her glass. "No."

"Ah."

That was all he said, just "ah." But as they ordered their meal and Brian selected a wine to go with it, Pat wondered about that "ah." Was it a statement? A question? A judgment?

Finding no answer to her questions, she grew annoyed with herself for asking them. After all, what did it matter to her what Brian Culler thought? In the unlikely event she should ever again become involved with anyone, it for damned sure wouldn't be an arrogant bass fisherman who'd never had a serious relationship in his life. So he could take his smug, know-it-all "ah" and dangle it in front of some other female. Pat Langston wasn't going to rise to the bait.

"What do you mean, 'ah'? " she blurted.

Leaning forward, he rested his chin on his hands and smiled that Big Bad Wolf smile at her. Startled by the pure sensuality in his look, she leaned back.

"Just, 'ah,' " he said. When she narrowed her eyes at him, his expression turned serious. "I suppose I mean that you're either still hurting from your divorce or you've decided all men are pond scum."

"Not that it's any of your business, but I'm not still hurting from my divorce. I've had four years to adjust to my single lifestyle and I like it fine. And," she added, "I don't think all men are scum, although it seems I run into the less-than-savory kind on a frequent basis."

"Are you saying that your line of work has something to do with the kind of men you meet?"

"Perhaps we'd better not discuss my 'line of work.'"

With the reflexes of a champion angler, he reached across the table and captured her hand. "Perhaps we'd better not," he agreed, his thumb stroking across her knuckles.

"You promised you'd behave," she reminded him, tugging her hand free so it could join her other one in her lap.

"I am behaving."

"Holding my hand is not behaving, Brian."

"I wasn't 'holding your hand,' I was offering comfort in your moment of distress. If I'd known you were so touchy about your divorce, I wouldn't have brought it up."

"I wasn't distressed," she protested, stifling the laughter his words and look encouraged. "And I'm not touchy about my divorce."

He let that sink in, nodding his head as he studied her from under lowered lashes. "So, you don't hate men, but you don't date. Why not?"

Wondering why he was pushing the issue, Pat studied her hands for a moment. She wanted to be exasperated with Brian, but couldn't find that emotion in her heart. His sharp wit and quick comebacks stimulated her in a way she found enjoyable. And as much as she hated to admit it, she was also enjoying his single-minded attention—she'd yet to catch him eyeing the other women in the place. As long as he didn't revert to anger, she could hold her own with him, she was certain.

But, she reminded herself, it didn't matter if she could hold her own with him. Just as it didn't matter if she was attracted to him or if he turned on lights inside her, mentally as well as physically. She wasn't in the market for a relationship. She only had to remember the first thirty years of her life and she'd keep her head on straight and her libido in line. And she merely had to lay it all on the line for Brian and he'd back off. She raised her head and met his dark gaze with a self-assured look.

"I'm thirty-four years old, Brian, and proud of it. I've given birth to two children, and I'm proud of that too. I'm not some impressionable young girl. In fact I'm probably one of the least impressionable people you'll ever meet." She paused, waiting for his reaction. When none was forthcoming, she went on. "I speak my mind, don't play games, and seem to be doing quite well on my own. But even if there were somebody I found interesting, I don't have time to date. I'm doing well to balance family and career."

To her surprise, he didn't argue with her. He

didn't even blink. He simply asked, "Did your ex resent your career?"

"Michael *was* my career," she stated before she could stop herself. "Which I thought we weren't going to discuss."

Brian arched his eyebrows, his curiosity eating holes in his patience. *Later*, he told himself, *as in some other night.* There'd been a certain amount of "ouch" in her voice, and tonight he wanted to keep things on an even keel—and Pat just a little off balance.

He wanted her to be curious about him, too, and since she hadn't asked, he'd volunteer. "We're not discussing your career. But mine has caused me problems with women, you know."

"So many women, so little time?"

Her remark drew a laugh from him. "More like too many tournaments and not enough time."

"Come on, Brian, my father was a tournament angler, remember? I know what goes on."

"What goes on?" He leaned back and crossed his arms over his chest, enjoying Pat's sudden vehemence.

"If you really want me to spell it out for you, I will. I know about the tournament groupies— blondes, redheads, brunettes, tall, short, skinny, plump, anything and everything you could want."

He started to point out that true groupies were

few and far between, but noting the determination in Pat's expression, he changed his mind. Looking upward, he pretended to think about it before asking, "What if I don't want?"

Her snort of disbelief caused a few people to glance at them, but she didn't seem to notice. "Every man wants, Brian. Especially when it's free, fun, and convenient."

Leaning forward, he propped his elbows on the table and rested his chin on his hands, withholding a chuckle when Pat automatically leaned back. "I don't think I like being lumped in your 'every man' category, and I don't think your father would either. As you said, he was a tournament angler too."

She opened her mouth to say something, then shut it, focusing her attention on the approaching waitress. While the woman set their entrees in front of them, Brian was aware of Pat's avoidance of his eyes.

More curious than ever, he chewed his first bite of steak while he watched her toy with her fish. He admired her attitude about casual sex, but he still didn't know why she didn't date. She'd said she didn't have time, but he knew that was an excuse.

He should know, he'd used that same excuse for the past couple of years. The truth was, he just hadn't met anyone who interested him enough to drag him out of his solitary lifestyle. So he told everyone he had to concentrate on his career, and he fished every tournament he could, living away from home five days of every week for six months of every year. In the off-season he worked trade shows for his sponsors on a twice-monthly basis. Only his family kept him home, those weekends when the Culler clan had something special planned. Casual dating was too much of a hassle.

Looking at Pat, he wondered if she felt the same way. Now that he thought about it, he could see where it might be even more of a hassle for a woman than it was for a man.

"How's the fish?" he asked, determined to be on good behavior for the rest of the evening.

"It's okay." Wincing, she added, "I mean, it's good."

He shook his head. "No. It's okay. Not bad for restaurant fish, but not as good as fresh."

"There's nothing as good as fresh fish, is there? Where you catch it, clean it, and cook it right there, on the spot."

"Did you do that with your—" Biting down on "ex," he substituted "father?"

When Pat launched into memories of her childhood, Brian watched her face, feeling warmed by her animation. Content to listen, he let her ramble, paying more attention to her expressions and gestures than to her words.

Responding to her appreciative audience, Pat threw herself into the retelling of the highlights of "growing up with P.J." She would never admit it to Brian, but in truth, P.J. had never grown up.

Before she knew where the time had gone, Brian was eating dessert and she was up to recent history with her P.J. biography. As always, she'd left out the bad stuff, the times when her father had been less than an exemplary provider for his family.

An auto mechanic by trade, P.J.'s love of fishing had often interfered with his wage earning. Granted, he'd been a pioneer in the world of modern, big-money fishing, starting as a guide long before guiding became a profession. It was also long before the career paid much money.

From Pat's perspective, *pioneer* translated into *poor*. Even with her mother's job in a sewing factory, there were lean times until P.J., working with Clive Cuthbertson, had produced his book on structure fishing. Pat had been in her last year of high school when the book catapulted her father to instant bass-fishing fame.

"Wow," she said, looking at Brian over her

wineglass. "I'm sorry. I got kind of cranked up, didn't I?"

"I enjoyed it," he insisted. "Is your father the reason you chose writing about outdoor sports?"

"Kind of," she hedged, her natural reluctance to talk about herself taking hold. But then she felt foolish. She would probably never see Brian Culler again after tonight.

"To be truthful, I just kind of fell into it," she admitted. "My ex-husband was editor of a weekly paper when I went to work for him as a summer intern after my sophomore year of college. I was aiming for a journalism degree at the time. He suggested I write a column, and the thing I knew the most about was fishing. After I married Michael that fall, I continued to write my column." Unable to contain a sigh, she leaned back in her chair. "Back then I wanted it all. A husband, family, and career." Brightening, she flashed a grin. "Oh well, two out of three ain't bad. Right?"

"Right."

"Of course for a while there it was the other two out of three. Husband and family, I mean."

"You didn't work"— Brian sought for the phrase he needed—"outside the home?"

"No. Michael didn't want me to work 'outside the home.' Besides, I had the twins to care for, and they were a real handful, believe me. I seemed to stay busy every minute of the day."

"I can imagine," he said, dismissing the urge to mention his twin brothers. He wanted to keep Pat talking. "So, your career wasn't a factor in your divorce?"

"No, it most certainly was not! In fact I guess you could say that my divorce created my career. Such as it is."

"Looks like you're doing pretty well. I'm surprised we haven't met before."

"As a rule I don't work tournaments."

"Why not? Seems like a great place for a writer to find stories."

"I, um, I'm usually too busy to manage the extended time involved."

He waited for more, but she focused her concentration on folding her napkin into a neat little square, ignoring his patient look. After several seconds of silence he shrugged and motioned to the waitress. Pat Langston had just closed shop on him, for reasons known only to her. But Brian hadn't become a champion fisherman without developing a huge reserve of patience and a certain appetite for challenge.

Relieved to have gotten through the dinner without any unpleasantness, Pat fell in step with Brian when he started toward her room. His embellished recollection of a major tournament goof he'd committed earlier that year carried them along, erasing her worries with mutual laughter.

She was still chuckling when they stopped at her door. "Thanks, Brian," she said. "I had a nice time."

"Me too." He rocked back on his heels, thumbs hooked into his pockets. "You're fun to be with, Pat."

Feeling like a schoolgirl on her first date, she lowered her head and stared at her sandals. And like a schoolgirl on her first date, she wondered if *he* was going to try to kiss her. She slid her key into the lock, uncertain about the regret she felt. She'd wanted Brian to behave, hadn't she?

She turned the knob without looking at him. "Good night, Brian, thanks again. And congratulations, again."

"Wait, Pat."

His hand covered hers. When she looked at him, her heart missed several beats under the power of his dark-eyed gaze.

"I don't want to get out of line," he said, "but I really liked the way you congratulated me earlier today."

She smiled. Slanting an impish look at him, she gave him her previous opening line. "How do you want to do this?"

Brian wasn't going through that whole process again, she learned an instant later.

"Like this," he murmured, sliding his arms around her.

Startled by the intensity his touch stirred in her, Pat wanted to protest, but when his mouth rocked over hers, she found herself caught in a storm of emotions. She'd asked for it, she thought hazily as he melted her with a warm, gentle magic that promised to fulfill fantasies she'd yet to imagine.

Brian tasted the sweetness he'd sampled earlier, teasing Pat's wonderfully distracting lips. Telling himself not to get out of line, he resisted the temptation when her lips parted, choosing instead to trail hot, wet kisses down her neck, down to the hollow of her throat. But when he worked his way back up, her soft moan set him on fire—and he allowed himself one long, slow, foray into her mouth.

And just that quickly he was no longer sure he could keep himself in line. He wanted to take this heady rush of pleasure to its limit.

In an effort to appease the passionate demon demanding relief, he slid his hands up over Pat's ribs, brushing the sides of her breasts with his thumbs. Although she gasped into his mouth, she didn't pull away. Her nipples tightened against his chest. Unable to contain the hunger, he deepened the kiss, seeking all the secrets of her mouth, exploring the sweet moistness. When the ache in his groin grew to explosive proportions, he reached behind her and opened the door, urging her into the room.

Pat tore her mouth free and stepped back, stopping Brian when he tried to follow her. As he reached for her again, she shook her head, feeling the rise and fall of his chest under her fingers as he dragged in ragged breaths that matched her own.

"I don't do one-night stands," she stammered, wondering if he would even hear her over the pounding of her heart.

"Neither do I," he said, his voice rough and husky. "But this—"

"But nothing. Good night." She reached for the door.

"Wait." He grabbed her wrist. "We can't leave it like this. There's something good and powerful between us. I can't believe you don't feel it."

Blinking back tears of shame, Pat looked up at the sky. In all the years she'd been married to Michael, she'd never felt this fiery kind of need. And she'd certainly never kissed him with such abandon. *But Brian's an expert at such things*, she reminded herself. *He's had plenty of practice.*

"I don't know what I feel," she admitted, tugging free of his light grip.

"I won't pretend I don't want to make love to you right now, but I understand if you think it's too soon," he argued reasonably. "I want to see you again. I'll come to Atlanta. We can have dinner."

She cringed. He probably thought one more meal would be the incentive for her to haul him off to bed and complete what she'd begun a few moments ago. "I don't think so, Brian."

"Why not? What just happened is a pretty good indication there's something special between us. We owe it to ourselves to find out what it is."

Refusing to look at him, she inched the door closed. "What just happened is a pretty good indication I drank too much wine." She'd had half a glass. "I'm sorry, I've already explained that I don't date."

He flattened his hand against the door with enough force to stop her from closing it. "You said you were too busy. But nobody's that busy."

"I am." Despite her fervent prayer that she would never run into him again, she didn't need to make an enemy of him. Realizing she'd sounded like a petulant five-year-old, Pat said in a softened tone, "You're a nice man—"

"Then say you'll have dinner with me next Saturday. Let's get to know each other."

"I'm really not interested. I'm sorry," she repeated.

Closing the door on the confusion in his eyes, she choked back a sob as shame overwhelmed her. *Why now?* she asked herself with bitter fury, struggling to contain her tears. Why, after thirty-four reasonably sane years, had she suddenly developed a case of raging hormones?

And why Brian Culler? If she had to get the hots for someone, why couldn't it be a nice, safe someone? Why did she have to get all stirred up by a professional bass fisherman, for Pete's sake? And a diehard bachelor to boot!

And then another thought staggered her. How long would it be before the entire fishing world knew how she'd behaved in Brian's arms?

FIVE

Although Pat was determined to ignore the roses that arrived at her house on the Monday after her return from Eufaula, her kids had other ideas. When she dragged herself to bed that night, the beautiful red buds were overflowing a crystal vase on her dresser. She glanced again at the card, shaking her head at the message: *Roses are red and smell better than bass. I hope you've forgiven this National Champ Ass. B. C.*

The note would have been much more humorous if it hadn't triggered an avalanche of questions from her children.

On Tuesday, when she saw the return address on the Express Mail box the postman delivered, she decided not to open it, but once again her plan was foiled. When one of her children spotted her sneaking out with it, Pat figured trashing it would stir more curiosity than opening it. It contained a bottle of imported wine and the message: *When you sippa this wine-a, I hope you'll recalla, the funna we hadda at old Lake Eufaula.* Explaining her smile was tough this time.

When the mail arrived on Wednesday, her daughter's excited whoop carried through the three walls that separated Pat's office from the front door.

"Whatcha get this time?" Leslie danced from one foot to the other while she waited for Pat to open the envelope. Inside were three tickets to the next Atlanta Symphony concert. Puzzled, Pat barely heard the kids' groans. Then she remembered, she'd told Brian she'd given birth to two babies.

Chuckling, she held up the tickets. "Who wants to go?" In a flash the children were out of the office.

Turning her attention to the note that accompanied the tickets, she frowned. *I've been told this music is something to hear, but I don't need concerts as long as you're near.* Like a good professional fisherman confronted with a stubborn Momma bass, Brian Culler was throwing every lure in his tackle box.

Sighing, Pat crumpled the note and dropped

it into the trash can. There was only one way to her heart, and no dedicated bachelor would ever negotiate that child-strewn path.

She was changing the water in the roses when Judd Braxton called the next morning. As a rule, she only heard from the tourney director when he had an assignment for her. This time was no exception. But she nearly dropped the phone when he mentioned a substantial sum of money.

"Say that again, Judd?"

"I asked if you were interested in earning a quick five thousand."

"You bet I am. What do I have to do?" Short of selling her body, Pat figured she was game for anything. She was wrong, she discovered in the next instant.

"It's pretty simple, really. You have to spend a week with Brian Culler."

She snatched the receiver from her ear as if she'd been burned, her initial excitement replaced by a strange terror as she remembered the feel of Brian's mouth on hers.

"I have to do what with whom?" she asked, pressing the cool plastic to her ear once more.

"You have to spend a week with Brian," Braxton repeated, chuckling before he went on. "Oh, you don't really have to spend a week with him as in 'spend' a week. You have to shadow him, though. And then you have to produce twenty thousand words on him for a book featuring the past five National Champions." He was quiet for a long moment. "Pat? You still there?"

"Uh-huh. Tell me again how much this job pays."

"Five thousand, on acceptance. Plus expenses. Stan Lofton was going to do it, but he signed a three-book deal with Woods Press. Kind of left us in the lurch, and our deadline is less than two months away." Judd paused, but when she didn't say anything, he spoke again. "What we're looking for is the man behind The Man. That's why we want you to spend some nonfishing time with Brian before you do the tournament thing."

Pat hesitated. The tournament thing meant two practice days and two tourney days in a boat with Brian, but she was certain he'd be no problem to her then. It was the "nonfishing" time that worried her.

In the end the money made the decision for her. "I'd love to do it, if Brian agrees," she said, trying to sound cheerful.

"I've already talked to him, and he wants to discuss it with you before he decides," Judd said. "Can you have dinner with him on Saturday?"

With her heart pounding in her chest, Pat realized Brian was trying to force his way into her life with the subtle tread of a brontosaurus. Her first instinct was to refuse to have dinner with him, even though it might cost her that fat writer's fee. But before she could speak, another idea brought a smile over her face. "Of course. Tell Brian I'll cook dinner for him Saturday. I'm sure he'd appreciate a home-cooked meal."

She'd learned one important lesson since her divorce at least. If there was one thing that could cool the ardor of a carefree bachelor, it was a healthy dose of children.

That day the mailman delivered three season passes to Atlanta's popular amusement park, Six Flags Over Georgia. The accompanying note warmed Pat's cheeks.

Strictly as a courtesy to Brian, she clipped a copy of her column about him from the previous day's paper to send him. With it she included a thank-you note acknowledging his gifts—and asking him to cease and desist. It took her longer to compose the note than it normally took to write an entire column.

Tamping down his anxiety, Brian knocked on Pat's door five minutes before the appointed hour on Saturday. Moments later, when he found himself being scrutinized by green eyes somewhat below the level of his own, he braced himself. His future chances with Pat probably rested in the hands of this pixie-faced little girl and her twin.

"Oh, wow," the girl said before he could decide how best to greet her. The "wow" was drawn out into two syllables.

"Hi," he ventured, aiming for the intelligence in those bright eyes. "I'm Brian Culler. I'm looking for Pat Langston?"

"Wow," the girl repeated, looking him over from head to toe. Brian silently thanked his sister and niece for selecting his clothes for the evening. At least one member of the Langston family seemed impressed by his dark slacks, white shirt, buckskin jacket, and conservative silk tie.

"I'm Leslie," the girl said when she finished her appraisal of him. "Come on in, Mr. Culler. The flowers and stuff were neat."

Stepping into the little foyer, he muttered, "I'm glad someone liked them."

"Mom liked them."

"She did?" he asked, recalling the polite but unenthusiastic note he'd received that morning. It was the only reason he wasn't laden with long-stemmed roses at the moment.

"Yes sir, but don't tell her I told you. Okay, Mr. Culler?"

"Okay," he agreed, adding, "Why don't you call me Brian?"

"I'll ask Mom." With a maturity that belied her size, Leslie led him across the slate-floored entryway and through an interior door.

"Mo-om!" she yelled toward another door, the volume of her singsong voice absurd in comparison with her small size. "Mr. Culler's here!" Then she turned her attention on him again, a demure little smile in place. "She'll be here in just a minute. If you'll excuse me, I have to set the table."

He looked around the room, pleased when he noticed the flowers he'd sent the previous day gracing a table. Pat had prudently removed the little card with its personal verse, Brian noted with a touch of pride. The flower-shop clerk, with whom he'd developed a telephone relationship, had agreed it was his best effort to date.

When a movement in the doorway caught his eye, he turned toward it, expecting to see Pat. Instead he found himself staring into the slightly antagonistic face of a lanky teenage boy. Under a shock of dark hair, gray eyes studied him as the youth approached, hand outstretched.

"I'm Grady Langston. You must be Brian Culler."

"Yes," he said. Looking into eyes nearly level with his own, he estimated Grady Langston to be fifteen, maybe sixteen. A visiting cousin? Brian wondered.

"Hi, Brian. I hope you didn't have any trouble finding us," Pat's voice rescued him from the awkward silence. As she bustled into the room, she wiped her hands on a dish towel. Noting her faded jeans and worn T-shirt, Brian dismissed his last little hope for a romantic dinner for two.

"No trouble," he assured her. "Bo's directions were very detailed, right down to the magnolia blossom painted on your mailbox." He'd wondered how she would act, if she would feel awkward, given the intensity of their last moments together. She seemed relaxed and in control, which was more than he could say for himself. Overriding his pleasure at seeing her again was the uncomfortable sensation of gray eyes burning into his back.

As if she'd read his mind, Pat looked past him and said, "Son, I think you'd better light the grill. Everything else is ready." When the boy left the room, Pat focused once again on Brian. "You probably get tired of steaks, so we decided to grill chicken. Grady makes a special sauce I think you'll like."

"Sounds good to me." Brian was busy trying to figure out how the twins and Grady fit the family she'd described.

"If you'll wait here, I'll let you know when it's ready." She paused in the doorway. "I'll have Leslie bring you a beer. Unless of course you'd rather have wine. I have a nice import—"

Brian shook his head. "Beer's fine. We'll save the wine for another time."

"You're quite a poet, aren't you?"

"Only when I'm inspired," he said, refusing to honor the light sarcasm in her tone.

Pat made it to the kitchen before she let her laughter burst free. The look on Brian's face had been priceless—worth every moment of anxiety she'd suffered while planning this evening.

"If it's all the same, I'd just as soon sit in here." His voice interrupted her hilarity, spinning her toward him, her amusement disappearing under the impact of his closeness. Less than three feet away, he lounged against the kitchen door, arms folded across his chest, one leg crooked over the other. Somewhere along the way he'd lost that fantastic buckskin jacket and loosened his tie. "Maybe I can help."

Flustered by the sight of him looking so comfortable in her home, she stammered a negative response while she rummaged in the refrigerator. What was she looking for?

Beer. That's right. Beer. Clutching a long-neck, she drew it out.

"I didn't know what brand to buy. I hope this is okay." She set the bottle and a frosted mug in front of him. He'd settled in a chair, his long legs stretched out under the inadequate kitchen table. Before she could step away, he enfolded her fingers in his and squeezed, his touch so gentle, she might have imagined it.

"Thanks for inviting me to your home," he said in a tone that reeked of sincerity.

Moving to the sink, she ran cold water over her hands, her thoughts scattering in several different directions at once. This wasn't going quite as she'd planned. Brian wasn't supposed to be able to heat her blood with a single touch. He wasn't supposed to be sitting in her kitchen, looking as if he belonged. Of course, she reminded herself, she still had an ace or two up her sleeve.

As if on cue, her oldest son's voice rang out from the dining room. "Mo-om!"

Wiping her hands, she tilted her head at Brian when Dusty, who was ninety seconds older than Grady, stopped just inside the kitchen door.

"Son, I'd like you to meet Mr. Culler. Brian, this is my son, Dusty."

Lurching to his feet, Brian stared at the same kid he'd met earlier. Was Pat trying to convince him she was crazy? As slender fingers slid into his palm, he took a closer look.

The other boy, "Grady," had been dressed in neatly pressed slacks and a button-down shirt. This kid was clad in ragged jeans and a grease-smeared T-shirt.

"Brian Culler," he said, smiling as he shook hands with Pat's second twin.

The boy looked him over, studying him as intently as any father of any teenage girl had ever studied a prospective caller. He looked as if he wanted to say something, but couldn't quite decide how to word it.

Brian knew exactly how the kid felt.

Turning his gaze on Pat, Dusty said, "I think I know what's wrong, but I can't fix it. I guess we'll have to call the garage."

"The car won't crank," Pat explained to Brian before answering her son. "Let's call the garage on Monday, okay? We don't have to go anywhere this weekend."

"Aw, Mom." He groaned. "I wanted to go to the mall tomorrow."

"Yeah, Mom, we wanted to go to the mall."

Wheeling toward the doorway, Brian stared at the squeaky-voiced newcomer, a younger boy he guessed to be about twelve. Watching the boy's face as blue eyes focused on him, he stifled a chuckle and extended his hand.

"Brian Culler."

"Scott Langston, sir," he said, not bothering to hide the unfriendly interest in his eyes.

"If you boys want to go to the mall, you'll have to find a ride," Pat interjected. There was too much tension in the room, she thought. Although she'd intended to shock Brian with her family, she'd warned the kids to mind their manners.

"How long before we eat?" Brian asked.

"About thirty minutes."

"Let's go look at that car, boys." Striding to the counter, he set his mug down and flashed a grin at Pat. "If we're not back before the chicken's ready, come get us."

"But you can't—" Her half-formed protest was aimed at an empty doorway.

"He sure is cute, Mom. I hope you go out with him lots." Leslie's words drew a growl of frustration from her mother.

Pat choked down another throaty sound when she went to tell "the boys" dinner was ready. Brian was bending over the car engine, his bare torso sweaty and grease-streaked. And all male, she noted when he straightened and faced her.

"Did you really drive this old heap to Eufaula?" he asked.

Tearing her gaze from the salt-and-pepper

curls on his chest, she looked at the raised hood of the car. "Yes, I did. I happen to like that old heap, Brian." Satisfied with his embarrassed grimace, she asked Dusty, "Find the problem?"

"Yes'm, the starter's shot," he said, wiping his hands on a dirty rag. "Brian says he'll help me fix it, if we can find the part tonight."

"We'll talk about it over dinner, all right?" Pat couldn't read the look that passed between her son and her guest, but she'd bet Brian had promised he'd handle any objections she had to his fixing her car. "Show *Mr.* Culler to the bathroom, will you, son?" she asked.

As he washed his hands, Brian grinned at his reflection in the mirror. If Pat had been trying to scare him off by exposing him to her family, she'd failed miserably. He admitted to being short on experience with babies and diapers, but he was right at home with teenage boys and cars.

Looking at the silver speckling his hair, he winced. He'd never intended to be single this long, but until five years ago he'd worked fifty-plus hours a week at the iron foundry and fished nearly every moment of his free time. The pursuit of his dream had been costly in terms of time, money, and relationships, but he'd never seriously considered giving up.

When he'd made the transition to full-time

fishing, he'd figured to settle down pretty quickly and start a family. He'd figured wrong, he was to learn. It seemed most of the women his age who interested him were more interested in their careers than in having a family.

But Pat was different, her family was obviously of utmost importance to her. If something serious developed between them, she'd probably welcome the chance to be a full-time mom. After he became the first three-time National Champ, he'd retire from fishing and they'd all live happily ever after.

With that warm image in his mind, Brian whistled his way into the dining room.

Pat said little during dinner, but due to the kids, Brian learned a great deal about the Langston family, starting with the male twins' history. Their mother had died when they were ten months old, and Pat had married their father about a year later. They were now just sixteen and Pat's adopted sons. The two babies Pat had given birth to were thirteen-year-old Scott and nine-year-old Leslie.

He also learned, through subtle but strong messages, that Pat believed her life to be complete as it was. And the sullen Grady made it clear he considered himself the man of the house.

It wasn't until after they'd eaten dinner and he'd helped Dusty replace the starter on Pat's old car that Brian finally found himself alone with the woman who'd haunted his dreams for the past week. Music drifted from somewhere upstairs while he sat in the kitchen once more, nursing a glass of iced tea.

Pat sat across from him, and he knew she was uncomfortable without her buffer of children. He also knew she'd be even more uncomfortable if he told her the real reason he'd failed to place in the tournament he'd just fished.

At dinner he'd told the kids his timing was off and Lady Luck had taken a shine to another competitor. The truth, however, was that Brian Culler had flat out been distracted by the memory of a warm, soft woman who'd melted in his arms. Instead of seeing in his mind the structure he was fishing, he'd seen Pat's impish green eyes and her adorable freckles, and he'd missed pulling in fish that a two-year-old could have boated.

"Thanks for a nice evening," he said, needing to say something. "It's been a long time since I had so much fun."

"It didn't turn out quite as I planned," Pat confessed, thinking of the two hours he'd spent fixing her car.

"I'll bet it didn't."

Catching the challenge in his tone, she raised her head. "What do you mean by that?"

"I mean that you thought this evening would scare me off," he suggested, his voice light but his eyes fixed on hers with a compelling intensity.

Pat swallowed hard. What was she supposed to do, tell him he was right? Or was she supposed to tell him she'd had to rewrite her column about him five times because she kept inserting words like *exciting* and *sexy* into it? Tell him he'd been the center of quite a few erotic dreams? Dreams in which he not only stripped her of her clothes but also consumed her identity with his vitality so that it became impossible to tell where he left off and she began.

"Well, it didn't work," he said, unaware of her struggle. "I like your family. And I like you, very much. So where do we go from here?"

Now *that* she could handle. "You're a nice man, Brian, but we don't 'go' anywhere. It's not you," she blurted when he arched his eyebrows. "I just don't want to get involved with anybody. Not now."

Tilting his head to one side, he considered her words for a moment. "If not now, when?"

Searching his face, she found nothing more than sincere longing. But when he leaned forward and covered her hand with his, she felt the kitchen shrinking around them, leaving very little oxygen for them to share.

Shrink-wrapped, she thought, unable to contain a rush of panic, barely able to take air into her lungs. *I'm going to be shrink-wrapped with this man, unable to breathe without inhaling him.*

"It's okay, Pat." His deep-throated chuckle opened an escape hatch in the gut-gripping fear enclosing her. "I won't push, I promise. I'd like to see you again, though, spend some time with you."

Her practical nature asserted itself. "If I take on the book assignment, we'll be together almost all day, every day, for a week."

"Do you want to do it?"

"Of course I want the assignment, but . . ."

"But you don't want to spend a week with me," he finished for her. "I'm not some sex-crazed maniac, Pat. I won't expect you to do anything you don't want to do."

Tugging her hand free, she stood and retreated to the sink, turning her back to him. "That's what scares me," she admitted.

There was a long silence before he spoke. "What scares you? Me?"

"No, dammit."

At her soft curse Brian catapulted across the room. He'd been aching all evening to touch her, and now seemed as good a time as any. But when she spun to face him, he hesitated.

"Why are you so afraid of me?" he whispered, watching while she struggled with the answer to his question.

"I'm not afraid of you," she finally said. "I'm afraid of what you make me feel."

Sighing with heartfelt relief, he slid his arms around her, enfolding her, resting his cheek against her hair. "What do I make you feel that's so terrible?"

"Things," she mumbled into his collar.

"But aren't they good things?" He ran his hands up her arms, felt her shudder. "Well, aren't they, Pat?"

"I don't know if they're good or bad. I only know I don't have time for them. There's no room in my life for . . . things, Brian. There are lots of women who would jump at the chance to—"

"I don't want lots of women," he murmured, tipping her chin up. "I want you."

When his lips claimed hers, Pat's ability to reason vanished in a warm, moist cloud of pleasure. And when he pulled her hard against him so that she could feel the strength behind his words, she clung to him as a drowning person would clutch a life ring.

Some foggy time later, when the singing of the telephone penetrated her consciousness, she wrenched her mouth from his, uncertain which of them was breathing hardest. When he glanced at the wall phone, she slipped out of his arms, grateful he didn't know that a house with teenagers was a house where adults never had to answer the phone.

Taking advantage of the moment, she hurried from the kitchen, straightening her blouse and patting her hair. The last was a useless gesture. In the heat of the past few minutes Brian's roving fingers had loosened the pins in her French twist.

When she stepped into the dining room, the mirror over the sideboard showed her a pink-cheeked, disheveled, glowing image of a woman she hardly recognized. The sight created confusion within her. One part of her wanted to giggle like a teenager and another part wanted to run away.

"You can't run from me forever." Brian's voice spun her toward him.

"I can try."

"But do you really want to?" When she didn't answer, he went on. "Do you really want to ignore what you feel when I touch you? Do you never want to be held, and kissed and—"

"Shhh! The kids." She looked up at the ceiling,

her cheeks burning as her body reacted to his words.

He shot a guilty look upward, too, whispering, "Sorry, I forgot."

"That's a luxury I can't afford," she reminded him, groping for control. "Please, let's get back to business."

"My pleasure," he said, his arms open as he stepped toward her, a lecherous grin on his face.

"No, you idiot, not that. *Business.* As in the book assignment." With her back against the wall, literally, Pat put out both hands to stop the steadily oncoming Brian. It wasn't until he laughed out loud that she realized he'd been teasing her, and then she was so relieved, she fell into his arms in a giggling heap.

"This is nice too," he said, sighing as he cradled her against him. "I'll do business with you anytime, Ms. Langston." Tightening his arms around her, he drew in a deep breath, one Pat felt all the way to her toes. "You feel so good in my arms, Patsy Jane McKinley Langston. I'm going to like working with you."

"You think I'm going to let you do this every night we're together?"

"I hope so." He planted a soft kiss on her forehead. "Oh, Lordy, I hope so."

"You might be disappointed, I—" The rest of

her words were lost in his mouth. Which was a good thing, since his crushing embrace prevented her from breathing. When he came up for air, she pushed him away, softening her action with a shaky smile. "It's late, Brian, and I've got a column to write tonight."

Dipping his head, he brushed his lips across hers once more. "Yeah, and I've got a three-hour drive ahead of me."

Bemused by pangs of regret, Pat followed him into the living room and watched while he lifted his jacket from the back of the sofa and slung it over his shoulder, his fingers in the collar.

"Thanks for fixing my car," she said, seeking safe ground. "I'm sure you saved me a big repair bill."

Culler shook his head, clamping down on the urge to suggest that she needed a new car. While they'd worked on the old clunker, he'd learned from Dusty that this sprawling two-story, four-bedroom house belonged to the twins. It had been paid for by their mother's insurance at the time of her death, and her will stipulated it was to be held in trust for them until they turned twenty-one. At that time they could sell it if they wanted, and the money would be theirs. Knowing that, Brian better understood Pat's fierce need for independence.

"Dusty had it figured out, he just didn't know how to fix it," he said when he sensed Pat waiting for some comment from him. "You've done a good job with your kids. They're all pretty neat."

"Even Grady?"

He hesitated, sensing worry behind the question. "Grady's heart's in the right place. He's concerned about you. That's an admirable quality, I'd say."

"He's always been the serious one, but since his father left, he's become even more intense," she said, smiling ruefully.

Nodding, Brian reached for her hand as she started toward the door, his heart missing a beat when her fingers curled around his. "The teen years are hard, and twins sometimes have a worse struggle than other kids. One's usually outgoing, the other introverted. You just have to love them for themselves, like other kids."

"Spoken like a true family man."

He stopped, waiting until she turned and looked at him before speaking. "Contrary to what you think, I haven't lived my entire life in a self-centered vacuum. My younger brothers are twins. And even though you haven't asked, I also have two sisters, both older than me. I even have a mother and father, a grandmother, some aunts, uncles, nieces, nephews, and cousins, who are very important to me."

Pat ducked her head. "I'm sorry, I was rude."

"It's okay," he assured her, cupping her chin and smiling when she raised her head. "That's part of getting to know each other, learning all this good stuff. And I really do want to get to know you, Ms. Langston."

"You are a glutton for punishment, aren't you?" Pat quipped, still ashamed of her thoughtless remark.

"Let's say I enjoy a challenge."

There was silence after that, a silence during which she found herself wondering if he would kiss her again. For the life of her, she didn't know if she was hoping he would or praying he wouldn't. Before her hormones could gain control of the situation, she opened the door. When Brian stepped through it, she followed him onto the stoop.

"Thanks again for a great evening," he said. "I'd ask you to have dinner with me next weekend, but I'm fishing in Texas. After that tournament I'll be going straight to the one in Missouri."

Remembering the reason he was there, she put her hand on his arm to stop him from leaving. "When do you want to get together on the book assignment?"

He thought about it for a moment. "Let's shoot for the Lake Chickamauga tournament, two weeks from now. That's not so far for you to travel, and you'll be able to see where I live when I'm not on the road. Background for the book of course," he added hastily. "Does that give you time to make arrangements for the kids?"

Pat nodded. "If they can't stay with their father that week, I'll work out something with my family." When Brian backed up a step, she followed, feeling as if there were some magnetic field pulling her to him. Something was wrong, she realized. Something was missing.

"You forgot something, Brian."

"Yeah," he agreed, leaning forward to slide his hand inside the door. "Thanks for reminding me."

The light went out an instant before his mouth found hers, but Pat could have sworn a star exploded, her reaction was so swift and heated. Although the kiss lasted mere seconds, it stirred her to an immediate and shocking need.

It's only physical attraction, she told herself when Brian sauntered to his car, his tuneless whistle drifting over his shoulder. *You don't have to change your life for him, and he's certainly not going to change his for you.*

Sighing, she returned Brian's wave as he drove away. And then she remembered what had been missing.

"You forgot your tie," she whispered, watching his tail lights grow smaller.

SIX

Struggling to contain her rage, Pat glared at the telephone, picturing yet again the smug smile she knew her ex-husband had had an hour earlier. He'd called to tell her he couldn't keep the kids after all because a business trip had just come up. Surely she could postpone her little trip, couldn't she? he'd asked. After all, she'd always claimed flexibility as a plus in her line of work.

He didn't give a damn that he'd left her in the lurch on the very day she was supposed to leave for Lake Chickamauga. For that, Pat could have strangled him, slowly and with great pleasure. He could have at least *sounded* sorry.

As a result of Michael's call, she'd had her ear glued to the phone for nearly an hour, unsuccessfully trying to locate someone to stay with the kids. Her parents were visiting relatives in Ohio, and her sisters had legitimate reasons for being unavailable. She'd even tried Bo, but he'd already paid his two-thousand-dollar entry fee for the Chickamauga tourney.

Muttering a low curse, she lifted the receiver again, knowing it would be nearly impossible to reschedule time for the book assignment. Brian's next two tournaments were halfway across the country, and she was running out of time on the deadline.

"Brian?" She hadn't expected him to answer on the first ring, and the sound of his voice nudged her with regret. Under the guise of finalizing their plans, he'd called her several times during the past two weeks, and somehow their conversations had managed to wander into personal backgrounds, likes, and dislikes. Considering their different lifestyles, Pat had been surprised to learn they shared a love of country music, mystery fiction, and New York-style cheesecake, among other things. She'd also been surprised that Brian always spent a few minutes talking with whichever Langston kid answered the phone.

After explaining her predicament, she listened to several moments of silence. When he spoke, his suggestion forced laughter from her.

"You're joking, of course!" She laughed again to emphasize the insanity of his proposal.

"No, I'm not joking. Bring 'em with you. I've got plenty of room, and my niece can stay here with them while we're out. Carrie's a very responsible eighteen," he promised, adding, "The kids'll enjoy the lake. Think of it as a mini-vacation for them."

"But Brian, we're talking about *four kids*!"

His chuckle set off pleasurable waves in her ear. "I remember."

Resting the receiver between her ear and shoulder, Pat crossed her arms and tapped her foot. "Okay. Joke's over."

"It isn't a joke. You want this assignment and I want you to write the story. You don't have anyone to help out with the kids—I do. Why don't you ask them if they'd like to come?"

She knew better than to ask the kids their opinions. They'd be packed and in the car in five minutes flat, maybe faster. "Last chance, Brian," she warned when she could think of no good reason to refuse his offer, but five thousand good ones for accepting it. "You've got ten seconds to change your mind."

It was the longest ten seconds of her life, and the quietest. And when it ended, Pat gave him an extra five seconds for good measure before she spoke again, her words spilling out on a big sigh. "Okay. Give me directions and prepare for the invasion."

That was how she came to be sitting in awed silence in front of Brian's house a little more than four hours later.

The weathered cypress siding beautifully complemented the woodlands surrounding the spraddle-legged U-shaped structure. Brian had described the house, telling her the two wings angled slightly inward, but he'd failed to mention the center section was primarily glass. That glass was now reflecting a breathtaking blue-and-green panorama of Lake Chickamauga.

From the majesty depicted on the lower level, Pat looked up at the second story atop the center, where two sets of French doors opened onto a narrow balcony. She managed a smile.

"Let's go storm the fort, gang." She wished she felt as confident as she sounded.

When the front door opened, she found herself staring at a dark-haired, dark-eyed young woman who looked younger than eighteen.

"Hi, I'm Carrie," the fresh-faced beauty said. "You must be Ms. Langston. Come on in. Uncle Brian went down to the boat house, but he'll be— Oh, here he comes."

Following the direction of Carrie's gaze, Pat noticed the boat house for the first time, but it wasn't the two-story structure that held her attention. It was the man walking toward them with long strides, his broad shoulders and narrow hips outlined by bright sunlight shimmering on the water behind him. In that instant she knew how Cinderella must have felt watching Prince Charming cross the ballroom floor.

Bounding up the steps, Brian spoke first to Leslie, then greeted Scott with a handshake before correctly naming each twin.

"Thanks for inviting us, Mr. Culler," Dusty said, extending his hand a fraction of a second before Grady's shot out.

"Thanks for coming. Your Mom and I really needed to get together this week. I just hope you won't get too bored while we work." Brian noted the enthusiasm in Dusty's handshake, the restraint in Grady's. "Since we're going to be together a lot, why don't you call me Brian?"

He smiled, knowing they were both surprised he'd gotten their names right. But it had been easy to identify the twin dressed in neat cotton shirt, crisp denims, and clean black Reeboks as Grady. Dusty was wearing a faded T-shirt, grease-spotted jeans, and dirty sneakers.

Turning to their mother, Brian felt his heart double-clutch. "Hello, Pat," he said in a casual tone, although he wasn't feeling the least bit casual. She was wearing a blue T-shirt tucked into tan shorts, and he couldn't stop his eyes from following the long line of her legs to her sandal-encased feet. "I see the old clunker made it," he added.

With her hands shoved in her pockets, Pat nodded, then tilted her head toward the house. "It's beautiful, Brian, really beautiful. And so's your niece."

"She sure is," Dusty mumbled, his cheeks turning red when everyone looked at him. Shuffling his feet, he looked down at the deck, then brought his head up, an embarrassed grin pasted on his face. "I, uh, I'm Dusty," he stammered, holding out his hand to Carrie.

The next few moments were mild pandemonium as introductions were made and the kids raced to the car to get their gear. Before they made it into the house, though, Brian nodded at an approaching boat.

"There's Travis. Carrie's brother," he added. "You all want to go in, or walk down there and meet him?"

"He's got his own boat?" Scott asked, eyeing the blue-and-white bass rig with obvious envy.

"He uses one of mine," Brian explained. "Why don't you drop your stuff here and go on down? He's expecting you, so just introduce yourselves."

When Leslie failed to follow her brothers, he squatted in front of her. "Tell you what, Leslie, why don't you let Carrie show you to your room? You'll be bunking with her, if that's okay."

"Oh, wow. That would be really neat, Mr. Culler." The young girl's smile stretched completely across her face. She happily followed Carrie into the house.

"She's always wished for a sister," Pat said into the sudden silence. "Are you sure Carrie won't mind? Leslie's a lot younger."

Brian shook his head. "There's a reason Carrie's the number-one babysitter in our family—she really likes younger children." Gesturing toward the water, he went on, "I asked Travis to come because he'll help entertain the boys. He's fourteen and"—he held up a hand to halt Pat's protest—"it'll be good for him, Pat. He's still adjusting to his father's death."

Looking at the cluster of boys huddled around the now-beached boat, Pat felt her heart to go out to Brian's nephew. "His father was your . . ."

"Brother-in-law," Culler supplied. "He was killed in a car accident nearly a year ago. Carrie's doing okay now, but Travis is still struggling. We've always been close, and that's helped, I think, but nobody can replace his father."

It was all said very simply, but Pat sensed a depth of concern behind the soft tone. "I'll tell the kids. And we'll try not to be too much trouble—"

"Don't tell the kids, okay?" he interrupted. "Travis needs to learn how to handle it for himself." Fixing her with a stern look, he went on, "And let's get something straight right now. I built this house for crowds, so I'm delighted to have the entire Langston crew here. If you say or do anything to make your kids feel like they're imposing, I'll never forgive you. Got it?"

Pat nodded. "Got it."

Against his better judgment, Brian cupped her chin and raised her face, sympathy gripping him when he saw the sheen of moisture in her eyes. "I didn't mean to make you cry."

She swiped at her tears. "Don't be nice to me, Brian. I can't take it right now."

Curling his fingers into a loose fist, he lowered his hand to his side instead of pulling her into his arms as everything in him urged him to do. He wasn't surprised to learn Ms. Pat Langston wasn't nearly as tough as she wanted everyone to believe. Someday he wanted to know why a woman who could hold her own in verbal battle cried when she was treated nicely. But right now he wanted to see her back in form, to see those eyes flashing instead of full of tears.

"I want to be more than nice to you," he whispered, raising his hand to cradle her chin again. "I want to make love to you. Soon."

Pat's eyes widened in shock, and she pulled her chin free of his fingers and stepped back. To cover the warmth his words poured into her, she countered his quiet statement with a flare of indignant anger.

"Look, Brian, I really want the book assignment, but I've also got to be Mom this week. If you can't handle that, I want to know right now." Glancing at her car, she wondered how long it would take to load her crew and skedaddle for home.

He chuckled. "Hey, I was only stating a fact. You turn me on, Pat. I haven't tried to hide that from you."

Narrowing her eyes, she caught the amused spark in his, realizing with relief he was deliberately teasing her back to normal. "Well," she said huffily, going along with the game, "I hope you're at least grown up enough to control your baser instincts while my children are present!"

Brian held up his hands with mock solemnity. "I would never say or do anything in front of your children to embarrass you." That said, he gestured her inside.

Stepping past him, Pat shooed away the image

of the spider inviting the fly into its parlor and concentrated on breathing.

In addition to being built for crowds, Brian's house, she soon realized, was also designed for easy living, despite its gleamingly clean surfaces. The center section was one huge room, combining a living area with open kitchen and dining area. The right wing of the house held two bedrooms joined by a bath, and they found Carrie and Leslie in one of those rooms, talking as if they'd known each other forever. The other room would be shared by Travis and Scott, Brian explained as he led her to the other wing.

Stopping in the only doorway on that side of the house, he motioned her past him. "You'll sleep here and I'll—"

"But this is your bedroom! I can't stay here!"

Hooking his thumbs in his jeans pockets, Brian leaned against the doorframe. "Please don't argue with me on this, Pat. My brain has good intentions, but I am, as you put it, 'grown up.' And what I feel when I'm close to you is a very grown-up thing."

"Stop talking about it!"

"Okay, then here's the deal. Leslie will room with Carrie, and Scott will room with Travis. The twins will have the upstairs rooms, and you'll have this one." Tilting his head back, he looked at her from under lowered lashes, his grin a sensuous white slash in his tanned face. "I will sleep in the boat house."

Pat opened her mouth to protest everything he'd said, then closed it, letting his last statement penetrate the fog in her brain. "You can't sleep in a boat house! The twins share a room at home, they can share one here. That way I can use one of the upstairs rooms."

"Those rooms have single beds in them, and the boat house is a bit more than just a boat house. It's a rather nice apartment. I moved some things in there after you—"

"Uncle Brian? Can we go skiing?"

Tearing her eyes from Brian's challenging gaze, Pat looked at the boy standing in the doorway. *A teenage Brian*, she thought immediately, smiling at the square chin that seemed out of place on such a young face.

The young boy was her height, and he wasn't nearly as hunkish as his uncle, but he would be one day, she felt sure. One day, when he'd matured and gained some character lines in that now-smooth face. When he'd grown some silver-white hair along his temples and on his chest.

Brian's voice interrupted her far-straying

thoughts. "This is my nephew, Travis. Trav, say hello to Ms. Langston."

"Hello, Ms. Langston," the boy said, flashing her a metallic grin before switching his attention back to his uncle. "We'll be careful."

"Why don't you let the boys take their stuff to their rooms first?"

"They're doing that now. I told 'em it'd be okay to change into swimsuits. So can we, Uncle Bri?"

"It's up to Ms. Langston," Brian said, tilting his head toward Pat.

Bemused by the idea of "Uncle Bri," she nodded her approval of the plan, smiling when Travis whooped his delight before trotting to the stairs.

"Feel better?" Brian whispered, drawing her eyes to his. "With all these kids around, we're safer than babies at a Grandma Convention."

"*Safe?*" Pat hissed at Brian as she stepped onto the boat a few hours later. "If this is your idea of safe, I don't want to live dangerously."

He shrugged in apology. "I didn't think it would be this tough." Looking down at his zipper, he added, "I haven't had this problem since I was a teenager."

Fixing her gaze to the top of his head, Pat bit down on the urge to tell him she'd *never* had this problem. "Well, you didn't make it any easier, walking around practically naked all afternoon," she pointed out.

Looking up, Brian lifted his hands in a frustrated gesture. "What did you want me to do, wear a suit and tie to go swimming? Besides, your swimsuit didn't leave much to the imagination."

"For your information, Brian Culler, that swimsuit is a modest one-piece. It shows nothing."

He grunted and plopped into the driver's seat. "Bare flesh isn't the only thing that can turn a man on. Having a pair of wet little bullets aimed at him can do it, too," he argued, looking pointedly at her breasts. "Why do you think I stayed in the water after the rest of you got out?"

Feeling her nipples tighten, Pat folded her arms across her chest and turned away. "Well, you could have put on some clothes when we played volleyball. I did."

"I knew I'd get all sweaty"—he paused when she groaned and slumped onto the casting platform at the front of the boat—"and we'd all end up back in the water to cool off. But for the record, watching your T-shirt slide up every time you went after the ball was no picnic for me. And hoping your shorts just would go ahead and split open wasn't fun, either."

"My shorts aren't that tight!"

Grunting again, Brian revved the motor. "If you don't want to find out just how tight those shorts are, you'd better stay up there." He added, "Because if you get any closer, I'll peel them off you, skin and all."

Pat ordered herself to concentrate on her work. After today the lake would be off-limits to Brian until the first practice day of the tournament. Recalling the heat she'd felt for most of the afternoon, she didn't want to think about the next two days, when he'd be forced to stay off the water.

Ten minutes later, after bouncing around on the bottom of the boat during a flat-on-top run across Chickamauga, Pat resettled herself on the casting platform. Refusing to be distracted by Brian's wind-rumpled hair, she said, "Okay, Mr. National Champ, let's get to work. When'd you start fishing?"

Without taking his eyes from the sonar unit mounted on the console, he replied, "When'd I start breathing?"

Pat waited for more, but he didn't add anything to the cryptic answer. Watching him, she realized he was truly caught up in his work, focused on the task of locating the fish he'd need in order to win the upcoming tournament. She wanted to see what he was seeing, to watch the blips on the sonar screen and scribbles on the paper graph, but she decided to stay put. Her shorts really weren't that tight, but Brian's threat had been deliciously real.

Although he was reluctant to talk about himself, she slowly pieced together his story, asking persistent questions while he motored over submerged drops and ledges.

Her admiration for Brian's success grew when she learned of his ten-year struggle to break out of his millwright's job at an iron foundry. He'd frequently put in sixty hours a week at his regular job, he said with a nonchalance that belied the difficulty of his accomplishments. Evenings and weekends he'd fished, studied fishing, or repaired his equipment. To her surprise, he confessed to going two years without placing in a tournament. Faced with such financial and personal sacrifice, most men would have become discouraged and quit, Pat knew. Brian admitted to being discouraged many times when his equipment failed or he didn't place in the tourneys. He also admitted to not knowing what had driven him so hard.

"I think I just wanted to be the best at something—anything—and bass fishing was my best shot," he said, shrugging away her praise. "I was okay at fixing machines, which was what I did back then, but I wanted to be really great at something. I wasn't good at sports in school, I was too shy and klutzy."

When Pat raised her eyebrows, he assured her it was true. "My earliest memories are of fishing with my grandfather, in the little creek at the end of our road. We kind of discovered bass fishing together, and he was the one who introduced me to P. J. McKinley's book on structure fishing. That book changed my life." He looked at her with such sincerity, Pat's laughter died in her throat.

The sun was setting when Brian finally turned the boat toward home. Grateful to have the day almost behind her, Pat remained in the front, confident they'd be able to handle their attraction to each other as long as they were careful to avoid contact.

Panic jolted Pat awake the next morning, her heart pounding even harder when she realized she really was in Brian's bed, just as she'd dreamed. Stretching out her hand, she breathed a sigh of relief. The dynamic Brian, who'd demonstrated an astounding amount of stamina in her dream, wasn't present. Hadn't been either, her hormones reminded her with well-placed twinges.

As she slid off the sheet, she vowed to wear her baggiest clothes all day and to don a T-shirt over her swimsuit if she went swimming. And to keep plenty of distance between her and Brian.

"And just don't look at him," she commanded herself as she rummaged through her clothes.

The last was easier said than done, she discovered, and keeping her distance didn't make her any less aware of him.

By the end of the day her nerves were frayed to the breaking point by her determination to hide her hormonal reaction to Brian Culler. All in all, though, she was proud of her diligence in the face of her inner conflict. If she could get through the campfire cookout the kids had planned, she'd have only one day left before tournament time. Brian, she was sure, wouldn't let anything distract him from winning the big money on his home lake. He'd forget all about her, she figured, when he launched his boat on the first practice day.

"Thirty-six hours," she muttered to herself in one of her rare moments alone as she pulled condiments from the refrigerator. "That won't be so tough."

But when she joined the little group already gathered around the fire, she realized it was going to be tougher than she'd thought. Whether by design or by accident, the only available seat was next to Brian. The other logs the kids had arranged around the fire were at maximum capacity.

Scanning the youthful faces, she wondered if issuing a motherly command for another seat would create greater problems than simply accepting her fate. Sitting next to Brian, staring at the colorful flames, and listening to the hungry little waves lapping at the shore sure seemed like asking for trouble.

"Come on, Mom," Scott urged, "Brian's already got a dog on a stick for ya."

Sighing, Pat trudged forward and eased down. Her first position, which left several inches between her and the man who heated her blood without benefit of fire, proved to be painfully punctuated by a limb knot. Shifting to her right, she bumped against Brian and almost fell off the log in her hurry to move away.

Chuckling softly, he slid his arm around her. "You gonna wiggle and squirm all night, woman, or are you gonna cook yourself a hot dog?" he asked, pretending exasperation. Pat knew he was pretending because he was stroking her arm while he spoke and each touch felt like lava on her skin.

Leaning forward, she reached for one of the straightened coat hangers he was holding in his free hand. "I'm going to cook and eat a half dozen hot dogs and a whole bag of marshmallows."

"You're going to cook my thigh if you don't quit rubbing against it," Brian murmured under his breath, smiling as he said to the group in general, "Anyone know any good ghost stories?"

Jerking her leg away from his, Pat concentrated on cooking her hot dog. When it was done, she could distance herself from Brian while she prepared the bun and fixed a plate of beans and potato chips.

Breathing in the tangy smell of wood smoke, she sat in silence, planning her strategy for the next day while the others talked. She didn't know how Brian felt, but she couldn't take another day of "family fun." Tomorrow she wouldn't go swimming and she'd find some plausible reason for not playing volleyball or engaging in any other potentially dangerous activities. Maybe she could fake some kind of minor illness, stay in bed— Brian's bed!—and read all day.

Congratulating herself on her wise planning, Pat pushed herself off the log before her hot dog was as well done as she liked. She had to get a head start on Brian so that they'd be in separate places for the rest of the evening.

After stumbling to the makeshift table laden with condiments, she heaped beans and chips on a plate. The kids were all gathered around, smearing mustard on buns and fighting over the ranch-flavored chips. Then she strolled to a log on the opposite side of the fire from Brian. As she sat, he stood, nodding his approval of her action.

Five minutes later Pat suppressed a groan. When the kids were all settled again, there was only one spot open for Brian. Next to her.

She didn't look at him when he ambled over.

Instead of sitting on Pat's log, Brian lowered himself to the ground and leaned against it, stretching out his legs toward the fire. No way was he going to subject himself to the torture of sitting close to her again. He'd told her they were safe, but that was before he'd spent half the night sitting on the boat-house steps, staring at his own bedroom window. It was also before he'd spent a whole day with Pat, listening to her laughter, watching a wet T-shirt mold itself to her each time she came up out of the water. And it was before he'd been forced to sit thigh-to-thigh with her and inhale that wonderfully distracting perfume. The heat he'd felt moments earlier was in no way attributable to the flames dancing a few feet away.

Shaking his head, he scolded himself for acting

like a randy teenager. He'd dated a former Miss Tennessee the previous year and she hadn't come close to firing his libido as Pat did.

This is ridiculous, you're a grown man, he admonished himself, *and Pat's a grown woman, with kids. The two of you have got to stop this!* But for the life of him, he couldn't figure out how to stop his body from overheating around her.

Biting into his hot dog, Brian decided it would be best if he avoided swimming tomorrow, and volleyball. And breathing, he added when Pat's leg brushed against his shoulder.

"Sorry," she muttered. "I was just trying to get comfortable."

"S'okay," he said, picturing her very comfortable, lying underneath him, naked and writhing and— "I think I need another dog." He leaped to his feet. He was glad Pat didn't point out that he hadn't finished eating his first one.

Digging a hot dog out of the pack, Brian wiped sweat off his brow. At this rate he'd need a cold shower before he went to bed.

"Cold shower, hell, you'd better dip yourself in ice cubes," he mumbled to himself, shoving the dog onto the wire. "Maybe you can play sick tomorrow, stay in the apartment all day. If you don't see her, you won't want her. Down boy," he grunted at the aching bulge beneath his zipper, "it's for the best, I promise."

"Uncle Brian?"

Lowering his plate to a strategic height, Brian turned to face Carrie, his cheeks growing warm as he realized she'd heard everything he'd said. "Yeah, hon?"

"Can we go out for pizza and a movie tomorrow night?"

"Hey, now that's a great idea!" He and Pat would be safe in a noisy, crowded restaurant, and he'd make sure they kept several kids between them at the theater. "Let's clear it with Pat."

"Okay, but we want to go by ourselves. Just us kids," Carrie went on. "It's more fun that way."

Brian had flirted with panic a few times in his life, but this was the first time he'd collided with it head-on. Leaving him alone with Pat was like leaving the fox to guard the henhouse. Swallowing hard, he forced himself to sound casual. "I don't know, hon. You're talking about quite a crowd."

"Don't you trust me, Uncle Bri?"

He thought about it for a moment, relief pushing through his concern when the answer came to him. "Sure I trust you, pretty girl, but Pat's got the final say-so."

And Pat, he was sure, would say no.

SEVEN

If a person could die from anticipation, Pat figured she was a prime candidate by the time Brian's black Blazer pulled from the drive the next evening. Instead of feeling guilty, she felt like she had the first time she'd known a boy was going to really kiss her—all fluttery inside, but eager for the experience.

She knew Brian was shocked by her decision to let the kids go out without them, but he hadn't created an opportunity to talk to her about it. In fact he'd seemed to take special pains to avoid her all day, satisfying himself with an occasional curious glance in her direction. Although she was dying to know what was going on behind those dark eyes, she'd kept her distance. She didn't need to flirt and play around with Brian to convince herself she wanted to have sex with him. All she had to do was look at him; her hormones did the rest.

She wouldn't let herself think of it as "making love." Brian Culler was a nice guy she liked a lot, but she was not in love with him. Being in love was too painful, too stifling. She was certain she was going to find being "in lust" much more to her liking.

When she switched her gaze from the top of the empty drive to the man who'd brought her to this junction in her life, she reminded herself that it was simple desire churning in her heart. Brian's obvious nervousness surprised her, but there was no denying the awkwardness in his stance or the uncertainty in his smile when he finally looked at her.

"I guess I'd better go study my maps," he said, shoving his fingers into his back pockets. "I'll just eat in the apartment."

"May I join you?"

He went still for so long that she wondered if her words had somehow frozen him in place. "Are you sure you want to?" he finally asked, his raspy voice having the most curious effect on her spine, and skin, and nerves.

She nodded. "I'm sure."

He sucked in a deep breath and looked away

for several moments. Exhaling, he looked at her again. "I've got some crackers and cheese and a nice bottle of wine, how's that sound for dinner?"

"Sounds great."

He stepped back without taking his eyes off her, and for a moment the raw hunger she saw in his gaze frightened her, but she managed a shaky smile.

"Give me twenty minutes to shower." His voice was a croak, and he had to clear his throat before adding, "Come over when you're ready." Grimacing, he rolled his eyes. "I mean—" He dipped his head and studied his sneakers.

There was nothing self-conscious in Pat's chuckle—she was enjoying his discomfort. "I think I know what you mean, Brian. See you in a few minutes."

She knew her boldness surprised him, but when she made up her mind to do something, she did it. Given the intensity of the physical attraction between them, they were going to have sex sooner or later. Carrie's request had cleared the way for it to be sooner, which was fine with Pat. She was ready to get it over with, to be done with this crazy hormonal turmoil and get her life back in order.

Ten interminable minutes later she slipped through the door to the apartment. She was standing in a compact living area, furnished with a loveseat and rocking chair and one small table. At the opposite end of the apartment was a double bed flanked by a dresser and by a door she assumed led to the bathroom. The two areas were separated by a tiny kitchen, a dining counter serving as the divider.

Fixing her gaze on the window over the bed, Pat waited. In only a moment the door opened, and a fully clothed Brian appeared, rubbing a towel over his hair.

He stopped when he saw her, said, "Excuse me," and disappeared again. When he reemerged seconds later, his hair was neatly combed, and Pat realized he wasn't quite fully clothed. He was barefoot and his shirt hung open, exposing the center of his fine chest and the salt-and-pepper curls arrowing down to his jeans.

"I'll get the wine." He padded toward her, fumbling with the bottom button on his shirt as he moved.

"Brian?" When he stopped in response to his name, she inhaled the warm, soapy scent of him. Longing to bury her face in those soft little coils on his chest, she whispered, "I don't want any wine."

His hands stilled on his shirt, and he simply stared at her for a long moment, his eyes smoldering with need. Then, as if he were afraid she might disappear if he moved too quickly, he raised his right hand and brought it to her face with infinitesimal slowness, lightly stroking his thumb over her lips.

"Your lips drive me crazy," he murmured, his grating tones teasing her fierce desire, his touch igniting her blood. Still staring at her lips, he lowered his head. "I think I should warn you, I've been walking around with a hard-on for the past forty-eight hours. I'd like to take this slow and easy and make it last forever, but I don't think I can. I want you too much."

"No more than I want you," Pat whispered, feeling a swift surge of pleasure when he groaned and pulled her against him. She'd never known this kind of power, this kind of heady hunger. She'd never before felt a man tremble—actually tremble—with the effort of containing his desire. And she'd never before known such caring as Brian demonstrated when he held her away and searched her face, his breathing strained.

"Sweet lady, please stop me now, if you're going to stop me at all."

"I'm not going to stop you, or me." She heard his breathing halt, saw him accept the conviction in her words, watched his eyes close, then open again.

And she was crushed against him, pressing against him as if she could weld herself to him. There were no more words, there were only sighs and soft moans, mingled with occasional low grunts signifying deeper levels of exploration. As the demand for gratification strengthened, the move to the bed was mutual and simultaneous, and somewhere along the way the light was flicked off and clothes were discarded.

And when Brian Culler slid into her, Pat Langston cried out, freed at last from the terrible anticipation that had held her captive for weeks.

Pat was on her second cup of coffee when Brian let himself into the house at four-thirty the next morning. This was a day she'd been longing for, the first practice day of the tournament, but now she found herself wishing she'd had more than six hours to recover her equilibrium. Uncertain about the proper behavior for the morning after, she stared into her coffee cup.

"Good morning," Brian whispered, making a beeline for the coffee maker.

"Good morning," she returned, her voice only slightly louder than the sound of liquid pouring into his mug. Although she knew he was looking at her, she refused to meet his eyes. She was afraid of what she might see in them now that they'd been as intimate as two people could be. And she was afraid of what he might see in hers, the new tenderness she felt for him, the absurd pride she'd never before known.

After their first, frantic need had been assuaged in an explosive few moments, Brian had taken his time, fondling her in places she'd never known were so erogenous, stroking her to life with gentle caresses and then satisfying her ravenous hunger. When she'd finally dragged herself from his bed, she'd felt completely fulfilled, emotionally, as well as physically.

Remembering her wish to get it over with, she allowed herself a silent huff of disgust. She'd truly believed having sex with him would lessen her attraction, that having shared his bed, her intense awareness of him would ease. Conscious of the familiar tugging between her thighs, she now knew she'd believed wrong.

"I heard the Blazer come in about midnight," Brian offered, turning to lean on the counter.

"Umm-hmm," she murmured. "The kids had a really great time."

"I'm glad, so did I." Gazing at Pat over the rim of his mug, Brian sucked down a long swallow of coffee. God, he wanted to kiss her! To just walk over there and pull her out of that chair and fuse her to him. His body still tingled from her touch, still yearned for more.

"Walking her home" last night, kissing her good night, and leaving her on the doorstep of his own house, had been one of the hardest things he'd ever done, but he'd known better than to come in with her. They would have ended up in his bed—the one in his bedroom in this house— and the kids might have found them together.

Sighing, he pushed himself away from the counter and shuffled toward the table. He had to work today, he couldn't stay here and look at Pat forever.

When he reached her side, he deposited his cup on the table and squatted beside her chair, placing his hand on her thigh with a gentle squeeze. "You okay? About us?"

The concern in his voice wrapped warm fingers around Pat's heart, and she nodded without speaking.

"Well, that makes one of us, I suppose."

Arching her eyebrows, Pat dared to look at him then. "You're not okay?"

His face split with the grin that always made her heart flop over. "I'm better than okay. In fact there's only one thing that could make me feel any better. And that would be to haul you back to bed and spend the next twelve hours loving you."

He paused, then corrected himself. "No, make that the next twelve *days*. We're good together, Pat. *Very good*, in case you hadn't noticed."

"I'm sure you would tire of me in less than twelve days." *And surely I would tire of you in that time*, she added silently, ignoring the lament of her libido.

"If you'd like to put your money where your mouth is, I'm all yours after the National," Brian countered, brushing his mouth over hers as he stood. "Meantime you want to watch me find some big old bass?"

Pat laughed in spite of herself, thankful he'd had enough practice at this kind of thing to know what to say to put her at ease. Having an experienced lover had its advantages, she was forced to admit.

The ride to the marina passed in companionable silence. Pat knew Brian's mind was already on the lake and his body was already standing in the front of the boat that was faithfully following them along the dark highway. Thinking about all the miles he'd driven in pursuit of his dream, she realized his odometer clicked off numbers more quickly than hers. Few people could claim that dubious distinction.

"There's Bo!" She couldn't keep the delight

from her voice when her friend's huge form emerged from the shadows while Brian was backing his rig into the water.

"Yeah, so I see." Brian's disgruntled tone surprised her, but before she could question him, he spoke again. "Can you park this thing for me?"

She looked at him in complete surprise. "If you want."

"Good. I'll back the boat off the trailer. Just find a spot wherever." With a quick movement he cupped her face in his hands and pressed a light kiss on her lips before he slipped from the Blazer, leaving her in stunned silence.

Shaking her head to clear her mind, she slid into the driver's seat, waited for Brian's signal, then released the hand brake and eased the Blazer away from the boat ramp, waving at Bo as she pulled up beside him. The big man didn't wait for an invitation.

"Well! Brian must really like you now," he insisted as he plopped into the passenger seat. "He's letting you drive this mean machine! I hope you realize this is tantamount to a proposal of marriage."

" 'Tantamount,' Bo?"

Dipping his head in embarrassment, he glanced at her, unable to hide his sheepish grin. Pat was one of the very few people who knew he held a Ph.D. in philosophy.

"Yes, 'tantamount.' It means—"

"I know what it means, but parking a man's vehicle does not mean 'love and marriage.' " She sang the last three words. "Only an ignorant, muscle-bound jock would think such a thing."

Grimacing in mock fear as she pulled the Blazer between two other vehicles, Bo waited until she turned off the motor before countering her statement. "Ahh, but you're wrong there. Only an ignorant, muscle-bound jock who knows Brian Culler as well as I do would think such a thing. What's going on, my old friend? You look . . . happy." His eloquent shrug told her he had chosen the word carefully.

"I'm always happy, Bo, you know that."

"You always *act* happy. This is something different."

She ducked her head and started to slide out, but he caught her arm and stopped her.

"Look at me, Patsy Jane."

She did, blazing heat at him over the use of her childhood name. But as she glared at the familiar blue eyes, she couldn't contain a smile. There was no way she could hide anything from the man from whom she'd contracted measles and chicken pox when they were kids.

Studying her expression, Bo nodded. "I'd say there's been a whole lot going on. Good for you." He was quiet for a second, then added, "Better for Brian. If he breaks your heart, just let me know. I've been looking for a reason to rearrange his face."

"He isn't going to break my heart. It's not that kind of—" Pat stopped, sending him a pleading look before speaking again. "Please, Bo, please, don't say anything to him. Or in front of him. Please?"

He held up both hands in surrender. "You know old Bo is the soul of discretion."

Pat rolled her eyes. "I seem to remember, Mr. Soul of Discretion, you were the one who told Jimmy Bradham I had a crush on him!"

Pulling his lips into a pout, Bo tried to look wounded by her opinion of him. "Well, little Jimmy was kind of slow on the uptake. And that was back in seventh grade!" he complained. In the next instant, he smiled with genuine pleasure. "I'm really happy for you, Pat. Brian's a nice guy."

Before she could tell him he was making too much of the whole thing, Bo was out of the vehicle and taking long strides to the dock area. She caught up to him and jogged along, answering his questions about the kids with a bit of extra enthusiasm, filling him in on the fun they were all having.

Brian heard Pat's laughter in time to look up and see her give Simpson a big bear hug.

"All set?" she asked—a little too chirpily, Brian thought. He grunted an affirmative without looking at her, pretending to be busy checking the drain plugs. But when she stepped onto the boat, he moved to help her, steadying her with a light grip on her arm. *Mistake.* The action brought his hand into contact with her breast, triggering a sharp pang in his groin.

"Be careful," she admonished, "that little bullet might be loaded."

Snatching his hand away as if she were a hot coal, he marched to the driver's seat. "No games today, Pat. I've got work to do."

I've got work to do, Pat mouthed at Brian's back, more amused than hurt by his brusque manner. So they were back to square one. Fine. She liked it better this way. She knew all the rules of this game.

Determined to ignore Brian's foul mood, she focused on the orange hues of the sunrise, watching the play of colors bouncing along the ripples on the water's surface. It was going to be a crystal-clear day, a "Brian Culler" day. When her host donned his goggles, she pulled on her helmet, still smiling with a newfound sense of well-being.

Expecting him to ignore her presence, she was surprised when Brian spoke to her as soon as he cut off the motor at his first preselected fishing site.

"What's between you and Bo?"

She finished stashing her helmet in her carryall before looking at him. "He's an old friend."

"What kind of 'old friend'?" Cupping her chin, he forced her to maintain eye contact.

Defiance flamed in Pat's chest, and she let some of the fire escape in the look she gave him. "It really isn't any of your business, Brian."

"Last night made it my business."

The words were made less harsh by his gentle tone, but they still bothered her. "Last night didn't change anything between us."

"The hell it didn't," he said, claiming her mouth when she opened it to argue.

When he raised his head several seconds later, Brian muttered a low curse and released her. With her lips pressed firmly together, Pat remained stiff, her eyes glinting like fiery emeralds. Cursing again, he stood, looking down at her while he sought a way to reach through her stubborn anger.

"You win," he finally stated, his voice low and

dead as he made his way to the front of the boat to begin fishing. He didn't want to explore the hurt he felt from knowing Pat had given him her body but not her trust.

Pat glared at Brian, angry with him for the way he'd asked his questions and with herself for making an issue of the whole thing.

"I've known Bo since we were toddlers," she said in a low tone. "His father died a few months after his family moved in next door to us, and my father kind of adopted Bo. He's been like a big brother to me, even though we're the same age, and we've just always been there for each other, through childhood traumas and adult crises. Nurturing each other through the divorce process made us even closer." Seeing Brian's shoulders slump, she waited until he turned to look at her before continuing. "Including you, I've had sex with two men in my entire life, Brian." She'd deliberately phrased it in blunt, unromantic terms. "Is that what you wanted to know?"

"I'm sorry. I had no right—"

"In these days of AIDS, everyone has a right—"

"Stop it, Pat. Don't cheapen what's between us."

She looked out across the water, tears stinging

her eyes as she stared unseeingly at the grayish blue expanse. "Go back to your fishing, Brian."

"No, dammit." It was a quiet refusal. Setting down the rod, Brian walked back to her, going down on one knee to put his face level with hers. "You're more important than any stupid fish."

The shock she felt was reflected on his face, so she remained silent, giving him time to correct his statement.

"I'm sorry," he said, holding her face with a feather-light grip. "I have no right to be jealous, but last night was really special to me. *You're* very special. Please say you believe that."

The humility in his voice stunned her, leaving her too weak to do anything other than utter an assurance of understanding. *Brian, jealous? Over her?* The idea didn't bear consideration.

"I hear a big Momma bass calling your name," she whispered, forcing a smile through the tears shimmering in her eyes.

Granting her a halfhearted smile, Brian brushed his mouth over hers. "Forgive me?"

"There's nothing to for—"

Tightening his grip, he graced her with a "charmer" grin. "If you don't forgive me, I'll jump overboard and swim in circles until I drown."

"Okay, I forgive you," she agreed, shaking off

his grip and giving him a genuine smile, grateful for his retreat to humor.

"How'd ya do, Brian?" Bo asked when they returned to the marina that afternoon. He was packing gear into the rod racks and dry-storage compartments of his boat when they motored into the slip next to his.

"I made out okay." He emphasized *made out*, and Bo looked at Pat, an unspoken question lighting his blue eyes. "Found a couple of little ones," Brian added with a nonchalant shrug. "How about you?"

Bo squinted. "I guess I found a couple of little ones too."

"Good for you." Brian dangled his keys in front of Pat. "Would you back the trailer in for me? I think we'll pull this old rig home tonight. I want to go over it one more time."

Pat's mouth fell open. Brian wanted her to back his boat trailer?

Realizing her mouth was hanging open, she shut it and took the keys, pushing aside the insane urge to ask Bo for assistance. Rising on wobbly legs, she took a deep breath and made her way to the front of the boat, thankful for Brian's steadying hand when she stepped onto the dock.

She hadn't backed a trailer in quite some time, but she resolved to do it right this time.

Since most of the other competitors were leaving their boats in the water, she had a clear shot at the ramp, and made it on the first try. When Brian drove the boat onto the trailer and motioned her forward, Pat was so proud of herself, she wanted to bounce in the seat.

After setting the hand brake, she slid to the passenger side of the Blazer, watching Brian through the rear windshield while he strapped down the boat in absentminded fashion, as if he could do it in his sleep. Allowing herself a quiet chuckle, Pat acknowledged he probably *could* do it in his sleep. His actions were reflexive, born of years of experience. Even his cursory glance at his trailer tires bespoke a man who knew his equipment and kept it in top-notch condition.

"Thanks," Brian said when he slid under the wheel. While he'd taken care of his boat, he'd searched for a way to compliment Pat on her competence. None of the women he'd ever known could back a boat trailer. He'd dallied longer than necessary, finally deciding to simply thank her as he would anyone who'd done him a favor. *You're learning*, he silently congratulated himself.

"You're welcome." Pat grinned broadly then. "It looks good, doesn't it?"

It was the first comment she'd made on his chances for winning the tournament, and he couldn't restrain an answering grin as he nodded. If the weather held, no one would come close to beating him.

"It looks real good, but I'm not ready to start counting chickens, or bass, yet. Competition's tough on this lake, and a lot of guys found fish today. Bo did well, so did Seth." He laughed when Pat arched her eyebrows. "Bo gets this tight little grin on his face when he's onto something really good," he answered the question in her eyes. "And Seth clams up. Only time that kid isn't babbling about something is when he's into fish. And I want you so much my teeth hurt."

The words were spoken in a conversational tone. They reached down inside Pat and flipped on a thermostat.

"I don't suppose you'd let me send the kids to town again tonight?"

The question made her laugh. "That would be just a little obvious, wouldn't it?"

"Yeah, I guess so." He squirmed in his seat, shooting a glance at his zipper. "Speaking of obvious. How do you do that?"

Pat followed the direction of his momentary gaze, then quickly looked out of her window. "Do what?"

"Make me want you without even touching me. Do you have any idea how hard it was—no pun intended—to ignore you today? How many times I thought about making love to you out there on the lake?"

"Stop it, Brian," she ordered, but it was too late. She was already imagining them lying naked in the boat, the sunshine beating down on them, the water rocking them while they explored each other as they had the night before. It took no effort at all to conjure up Brian's muscular torso and long, sturdy legs. And if she closed her eyes, she could see his fine, sensitive hands—

"Pat?"

"Hmmm?"

"I asked if you had any ideas."

Oh, she had ideas all right. But she didn't know how she could bring them to fruition, given the houseful of kids waiting for them.

And she really had to quit acting like a sex-crazed teenager. Opening her eyes, she cleared her throat and asked, "How about cold showers?"

His full-throated laughter jolted her from her hazy thoughts. "I was talking about buying Carrie something special when she leaves for college next month. I asked if you had any ideas about what I could give her."

With effort Pat made the switch in topics. "You mean in addition to paying her tuition?"

Brian glanced at her, surprise evident on his face. Looking back at the road, he grumbled, "That's supposed to be a family secret." And then he shot her a stern look. "And it's not for publication."

Chuckling, she nodded. "I know, '*Uncle Bri.*' I also know you're paying for Travis's braces."

"Damn," he muttered without looking at her again. "I'm scared to ask what else you know."

"I know their mother is very special to you."

"Now, that's no secret, but she's just a little more special than my other sister. Marilyn is only eleven months older than me, so we've always been extra-close. She's had a hard time of it since Sammy died—he didn't have much insurance—but she's stubborn about letting the rest of us help out." Slanting another look at Pat, he added, "She's real independent, like someone else I know."

She let the remark pass. "Carrie and Travis spend a lot of time with you, don't they?"

He nodded. "When I'm home. I took Trav with me to a couple of tackle shows this year, during the off-season. Don't know if it helped, but he seemed to enjoy them."

When Brian lapsed into silence, Pat's thoughts flowed naturally from the fatherless Carrie and

Travis to her own children. She knew there were times when they needed the kind of guidance only a father could offer, but Michael was more pal than male role model. Without really trying, Brian was a much stronger parental figure, handling all the kids with a firm sense of discipline balanced with tenderness and concern.

Thinking about the way he'd steadied Leslie when she was learning to ski and the extra, but thwarted, efforts he made toward Grady, she shook her head.

Brian caught the motion and glanced at her. "What?" he asked.

"How much sleep do you need tonight?"

"Sleep?" Seconds later he grinned as he understood the question. "Who needs sleep?"

Pat waited until well after midnight, until the house was dark and quiet and she was sure the kids were all asleep, before making her way to the apartment. When she reached the bed, she realized Brian was also asleep.

Taking advantage of his stillness, she knelt and studied his face, memorizing each feature, from the rumpled hair falling onto his forehead, to the thick lashes hiding the ebony eyes, to the freshly shaved, squarish chin. He smelled like soap and something else—something so undeniably male, it made her ache when she inhaled.

And he looked as energetic in sleep as he did when he was awake, she decided. *No innocence here, just pure virility.*

He was lying on his stomach, his torso bare, the sheet draped over his buttocks, his lax state inviting her to look her fill. With her fingers itching to caress the strength in his back, she admired the shape of the hair-roughened calf crooked toward her.

"If I'm dreaming, don't wake me up." Brian's voice was thick with sleep, but his arm was quick to reach out and encircle her. While his lips sought hers, Pat fitted herself against him as if she'd found the sanctuary she'd been seeking all her life.

Nearly an hour later she inched out from under the sturdy leg pinning her in place, trying not to awaken the once-again sleeping Champ. She made it to the edge of the bed before Brian's arm snaked around her middle.

"I have to go," she protested quietly.

"No, you don't," he argued. "You can stay with me. The kids won't know, we'll be gone hours before they wake up. I like having you here."

Blinking back tears, Pat shook her head and pushed his arm away. She'd managed to talk herself into having sex with Brian Culler, but she wasn't ready to actually sleep with him. There was something too intimate about falling asleep in someone's arms—something she was certain the vastly experienced Brian wouldn't understand.

EIGHT

Worried by Bo Simpson's tight little grin and Seth Henderson's ominous silence, Brian scowled down at the fish in his livewell. The lead he'd started with this morning, added to the bass he was looking at now should win the first-place prize of fifteen thousand dollars that this local qualifying tournament offered. But he knew there were no guarantees in tournament fishing.

Rubbing his neck to ease the tension there, he shot a frustrated glance at Pat. The week that had flown by much too quickly had left him with deep feelings for her and her family, and he wasn't looking forward to the stillness of his house this evening. Carrie and Travis had already left for home, and Pat and her kids would be leaving after the tournament.

Watching her tuck her notebook into the

hideous yellow bag, he realized she'd managed to pull his life story from him, but he still knew very little about her.

Granted, he'd seen her stirring pots in his kitchen and he'd felt her exploding under his touch, but he also wanted to see her tapping her keyboard and feel her sleeping in his arms. During the past week he'd discovered that she was a wonderful mother, a delightful companion, and an exciting lover, but he wanted to know more. He wanted to know why any man would walk away from Pat and her kids, and he wanted to know why she'd hoped this week with him would kill his interest in her, because it hadn't. He was more attracted to her than ever.

He'd made love with other women, but he'd never felt the sense of belonging, of "homecoming" that he felt with Pat. They fit together so well, seeming to want the same things at the same moment. Even more than that, she excited him on a level he'd never known before, in a way that tied him into a more complete person than he'd ever been before. But every time he'd tried to tell her how he felt, she'd quickly changed the subject, most often interjecting tales of the kids between them.

Great, Brian. Here you are, waiting to win or lose

on your home lake, and all you can think about is Pat.
He flipped up the lid of his livewell once more, frowning when a cheer went up from the crowd at the platform.

"Sounds like Bo really impressed everybody," Pat ventured, too aware of Brian's scowl.

"Yeah, I knew he'd do well. He nearly beat me the last time we fished this lake." Turning his head, Brian nodded at Henderson, who maneuvered his boat onto the waiting trailer. "And Seth's too quiet for my liking."

"It'll be okay. You had a great day." She didn't add that he looked as if he might collapse from exhaustion at any minute. Guiltily she remembered their explosive lovemaking in the wee hours of the morning. At least Brian would get a good night's sleep tonight.

"You don't have to go home today, you could stay over the weekend."

Brian's words brought her gaze to his and a frown to her face. So far she'd avoided talking with him about what might or might not be between them, and she wanted to keep it that way.

"I'm not going home today," she replied, bracing herself for his reaction to her next words. She hadn't even told the kids her plans, hoping to delay this moment as long as possible. "Bo's taking the kids back to Atlanta, and I'm staying here, in a motel. I'm fishing with Seth tomorrow," she explained when Brian's jaw dropped.

He marched back to where she sat, glaring down at her as he demanded, "When the hell did all this come about?"

"Yesterday."

Shoving his fingers in his back pockets, he narrowed his eyes. "I thought we—" He stopped and looked out across the water. After a few seconds he tried again. "I thought we had something special. I thought you might even—" He shrugged.

Finding it difficult to remain seated in the face of his confusion, Pat rushed her explanation, her voice sounding defensive even to her. "I'm a hook-and-bullet writer, Brian, which means I write about people who fish and hunt. Whether you like it or not, Seth is a story."

"I thought *I* was your story."

Lowering her head to escape the heat in his eyes, she nodded. "You *are* a story, but I have a weekly syndicated column that consumes material as fast as I can find it. One of the papers that carries my column is in northern Alabama, where Seth is from. He'll make good copy."

"He's an arrogant little smart-ass who gets lucky now and then." Ignoring the shock on her face, Brian made a sweeping gesture. "I can't believe you're going to write about him. There are so many better fishermen here."

Pat tipped her head back and counted fluffy clouds while she struggled with her temper. When she leveled her gaze on Brian again, she enunciated each word with great care. "It doesn't matter what you or I think of Seth. He fishes for a living, he's not doing too badly this year, and he's a story I need."

Further argument was delayed when the tournament staffer at the loading ramp shouted Brian's name. Stepping past her, Brian sank into the driver's seat. "Why a motel? And why Bo? You and the kids can stay at the house. For that matter, you could have told me all this was going on." The last was an accusation.

Jerking her thigh away from his, Pat curled her fingers into her palms and raised her voice to be heard over the drone of the motor. "I came to Chickamauga to gather material for the book, and that assignment ends with the weigh-in today. I wouldn't feel right staying at your house while I worked on another assign—"

"Is that all I am to you? *An assignment?*"

"I certainly wouldn't ask you to baby-sit while I was out working," Pat said quickly.

Seething, Brian bit down on a cutting remark and eased the boat onto the trailer. With his thoughts a jumbled mass and his gut churning, he barely heard Pat's "Don't worry, you've got it wrapped" when she stepped from the boat.

Yeah, he thought moments later when he loaded his fish onto the scales, he had it wrapped all right. Problem was, it wasn't wrapped tight enough. And neither was he, it seemed. He felt like someone had tugged on the wrong string and everything was coming loose.

As soon as the digital readout steadied, Brian stepped from the platform and wedged through the crowd, heading for his Blazer. He knew everyone would think he was upset about ending up in third place, but that wasn't the impetus behind his retreat from the noise. While he wasn't happy about losing on his home lake, he didn't begrudge Bo Simpson the win. It was Seth Henderson's second-place status that weighed heaviest on Brian's mind. And his heart.

Knowing the kid would like nothing more than to replace Brian Culler as National Champ was one thing, but thinking that Henderson would also like to replace Brian in Pat's bed was another.

Keeping a close watch on Brian, Pat applauded Bo's success. "Congratulations!" she exclaimed when he lifted her off her feet and whirled her around.

"Thanks, but I know you were really pulling

for old Brian over there." Lowering her to the ground, he wrinkled his brow as he took in the dark mood evident in the other man's actions. "He doesn't like to lose, does he?"

"Neither do you, as I recall." She didn't want to defend Brian, but the words just slipped out. "And this one is really tough on him, this being his home lake and all."

"You two still together?"

"Bo!" She punched his arm, shooting a cautious look at the other man, even though Brian was too far away to overhear. "We are not together."

Bo's chuckle warmed her cheeks. "You forget, I've known you since you were two years old, and I've come to know Brian pretty good while I've been eating his dust these past three years. You're in love with the man, my friend. And he's in love with you."

Pat's hand flew to her hips. "That's a load of horse puckey! Brian is *not* in love with me." Too late she realized she hadn't denied her feelings for Brian.

In response Bo shrugged and canted his head to one side, giving her a "tell it to someone else" expression. And then, staring over her shoulder, his eyes rounded in surprise. "Looks like your ride is about to leave, pretty lady."

Pat spun toward the Blazer, a gasp of disbelief escaping her before she spurted across the parking lot. She reached the familiar black vehicle as it rolled forward. With a fury born of sheer disbelief, she yanked the door open, blasting Brian with her anger at the same instant he braked the Blazer.

"What the hell are you doing?"

"I'm going home."

Pat blinked, confused by his calm manner. "You were going to *leave* me here?"

Shrugging, he looked out the windshield. "I figured you'd planned to ride with Bo. Or maybe with Seth, since he's your next *assignment*."

"You're jealous!" she cried. "Because I'm going to write about Seth! That's what this is all about, isn't it?"

Slowly turning to look at her, he studied her face, the sadness in his dark eyes tugging at her heart. "No, Pat," he answered in a low, tired voice, "that's not what this is all about."

"Then what's going on?"

"I'm not real sure," he admitted, his tone reflecting some inner misery.

A little more than an hour later Pat watched with mixed feelings when Bo's van pulled away from the lake house. This time was heartbreakingly different from the last time she'd been left alone with Brian.

Although he seemed to be over his bad temper, he'd made only minimal comments to her while helping the kids load their gear. Knowing he was unhappy with her decision to fish with Seth tomorrow, she could think of nothing to say to lessen the strain between them. She couldn't let Brian's antiquated attitude keep her from doing her job.

"I didn't get a chance to tell you," she started, clearing her throat before continuing. "I'm sorry about the tournament. I know it was really important to you."

Brian looked down at the circle he was drawing in the sand with his foot. "It's going to be tough staying out in front until the National. Point totals that qualify in other divisions don't cut it in the Southeastern."

Measuring the considerable amount of worry in his casual statements, Pat ventured, "And if you don't make it to the National?" Her heart went out to him when panic flickered across his strong features. "There's always next year, you know."

Shaking his head, he gave her a flat, despairing look. "When I started fishing professionally, I set a goal. I was going to win the National. And when I achieved that goal last year, I set a new goal. I'm going to be the first three-time champ." Turning his head toward the lake, he plowed his fingers through his hair, his gaze moving restlessly across the water. "I'm thirty-seven years old, and the young boys are on my heels like hound dogs after a rabbit. I know only one way to do this—stay out in front of the pack. If I ever let them overtake me, I'll be eating dust for the rest of my life."

"Well, then, you'll stay out in front," she stated, forcing confidence into her voice. "If anyone can do it, you can. You didn't get to be the Champ by being lucky, you're good at what you do."

He was silent for a long time before he looked at her again. "Thank you."

"For what?"

Reaching across the space separating them, he gently enfolded her fingers in his. "For not trying to rationalize away my fears."

"Fears are not always rational, Brian." She should know. She felt an irrational fear right now, a storm of confusion stemming from his touch. It was the same old battle she'd been fighting since the night they'd met. On a very primal, elemental level, she wanted to hold on to Brian Culler and never let him go. On another level, the intellectual one, she wanted to stay as far away from him as possible.

"I, uh, I guess I'm ready to leave," she stammered, regret filling her when she tugged her hand free. She was really going to miss Brian, she realized with a shock. Her days suddenly looked empty. With difficulty, she kept her tone light. "You've been really great to me and the kids. Maybe I can repay you someday."

"Stay with me tonight."

The soft request took her breath away, reminding her of the danger in prolonging the affair. "I'm sorry, but I can't."

Leaning back against the driver's door of her car, he studied her face with stubborn determination. "Can't or don't want to?"

Shrugging, she looked out across the blue expanse of water. "There's no reason for me to stay."

"Yes, there is. Please, look at me, Pat."

She did and her heart plunged.

"Dammit all, woman, I wanted to do this right." He grumbled, suddenly pushing himself off the car. When she backed away, he followed, matching her step for slow step. "I wanted candlelight and soft music and wine, but here goes." He drew in a deep breath, then let it out slowly. "I'm in love with you, Patsy Jane McKinley Langston."

Suddenly Pat's legs became solid chunks of lead, too heavy for her to move. *Run!* her mind ordered when Brian reached for her. *No,* her body refused, resting against Brian's hard thighs.

"You're not in love with me," she managed to protest. "It's only—"

"It's only the most wonderful thing that's ever happened to me." Brian's contented sigh tickled her hair. "Marry me."

Shocked, Pat leaned away from him. "You're crazy!"

"No, I'm not. We're good together—in bed and out—"

"There's more to marriage than that."

"I know, but if we love each other—" He stopped and searched her eyes. "You do love me, don't you?"

Swallowing hard, Pat lowered her head. "Maybe a little," she hedged, freeing herself from his arms and backing up a step. "But loving someone doesn't make the problems go away."

He frowned. "What problems?"

"You're a *bachelor*, for Pete's sake!" she blurted. "You've never made a commitment to anyone, never lived with anyone on a day-to-day basis." Seeing his frown deepen, she added, "Have you?"

"Well, no," he admitted, hooking his thumbs

into his pockets. "But I thought my single status was a plus. At least I'm not carrying around a bunch of garbage from a failed relationship."

The words heated Pat's blood. "And I am?"

Brian shrugged, his eyes wary now. "A little, but that's part of what's made you so strong."

Remembering their first meeting, she snorted in disbelief. "And you like strong women, right?"

"I guess so, I like *you*. I like your sense of humor and your sharp wit, and I especially like your commitment to your family. I like the way you don't let people run over you and you're always your own person." Smiling, he added, "If we were married, you wouldn't have to work, you know. I'm in good shape financially."

"Let me get this straight." Offering him her sweetest smile, she baited the hook. "You'd want me to quit work?"

"Sure. You could stay home and take care of the house and kids and not worry about the bills. You could maybe even have my baby." On that note his lips twisted in an idiotic little grin.

Nodding sagely, Pat counted to ten before she said, "Sorry, Brian, you'll have to find someone else to be your little wifey. *If* I were to marry you, and *if* I were to have your baby, I'd still pursue my career. But none of that's going to happen, I can assure you."

Moving toward her, he shrugged again. "So, you'll keep working, that's okay." When her eyebrows shot upward, he quickly amended, "It's better than okay, it's great."

"Like my fishing with Seth tomorrow is great?"

"Yeah," Brian said reluctantly. "I understand that you need a story."

"Do you, really? And will you understand when my need for a story requires me to spend three days in a primitive deer camp with a bunch of men?"

His chin went up an inch and his eyes narrowed, but he nodded. "Yeah, I'll understand."

"Oh, come off it. You pitched a fit about my spending a few hours with Seth. You'd never be able to handle some of the other stuff I do."

"I'll handle it." Pat noticed Brian's lips didn't move when he said those words. He glared at her for a moment longer before twisting his head to one side and rubbing the back of his neck. "I'll admit it won't be easy, but if I wanted life to be easy, I wouldn't fish for a living."

Pat's exasperation had grown to explosive levels. "That's another thing! We both travel too much. Relationships are hard enough when both people work normal jobs."

"We can travel together sometimes, you know."

"You're forgetting something, Brian. *Four* somethings, to be exact."

"The kids? I'm crazy about them, and they like me too. Grady will come around," he added before Pat could point out at least one member of the Langston family he'd misjudged. "We'd just have to adjust our schedules."

"I spent ten years 'adjusting my schedule,' " she countered, "and it didn't seem to make a difference."

"Okay, so I'll adjust *my* schedule. It can work, Pat. Like I said, I'm crazy about the kids."

Sighing, she put her hands to her hips and gave him her Mother-knows-best look. "Being crazy about them isn't the same as being a full-time father. This hasn't been a normal week. It's been like a vacation. You wouldn't last three days alone with them under normal circumstances."

"Try me," Brian suggested in a voice so reasonable, it grated like chalk on a blackboard. "The next time you have to travel, let me stay with the kids." When she raised her hands in frustration, he went on, "What's the matter? Scared I'll pass the test? Afraid you'll lose your excuse for refusing to get involved with me?"

He paused, but when she didn't say anything, he continued in softer tones. "Deny it all you want, sweet lady, but you're already involved with me. You'd never have gone to bed with me if you didn't feel something pretty special for me."

Lifting her chin, Pat maintained eye contact. "All right," she said, unsettled by the tumult of feelings she'd encountered in the past few minutes. "I have to go to a writer's conference next weekend. Oh, but you're fishing in Arkansas, aren't you?"

"Not anymore."

She stomped her foot, wincing when her heel landed on a stone. "You've already paid your fees and you can't afford to miss a tournament. You've only got five more weeks to qualify."

Waving away her arguments, Brian leaned forward with steely-eyed determination. "You *are* scared, aren't you? Damn Michael Langston!"

Confused, Pat frowned. "What's Michael got to do with this?"

"Isn't he the bastard who hurt you so much, you'll never trust another man? What did he do to you anyway? What do I have to do to prove I'm not like him?"

Hearing the desperation in Brian's voice, Pat knew she owed him some answers. She looked out at the lake while editing her tawdry little tale to its bare essentials.

"I spent ten years being Michael Langston's good little wife, cooking, cleaning, caring for the kids, *adjusting my schedule*," she started. "One day he decided he didn't want to live with us anymore. He needed space, he said, and we were choking him." Blinking back tears, she shook her head. "I'd been unhappy for a long time, so you see, Michael didn't do anything that terrible to me. And I already know you're not like him."

Brian was quiet for a long time before asking, "Then what's the problem? Why won't you even consider a future with me?"

"You're a *professional fisherman*! You live on the road."

"I've already said I'd adjust my schedule, travel—"

"You know that's not the problem," she cut in.

"Well, then, tell me what is!" he shouted, catapulting himself toward her with a speed that left her cringing in his arms. "Please, Pat," he whispered, "please tell me the real reason you're running from me."

She fought the pain she'd never shared with anyone, adding guilt to her burden when she realized Brian was really suffering. It wasn't going to be easy, but she had to make him understand why she could never let herself love him fully. Taking several deep breaths, she fought to steady her voice.

"I practically worshiped my father," she began, choking back a cry as agony swelled within her. When Brian's hands slid to her back, she nestled against his chest and gathered strength from the comfort he offered. "P.J.'s a lot of fun, like a big kid," she mumbled against his shirt. "He was popular at tournaments, a real party guy, but I never felt I was in the way when I traveled with him. I was in college when he went to the National the first time, but I decided to cut classes and surprise him." Despite her attempt at detachment, a bitter laugh escaped Pat. "*I* was the one who was surprised. He was entertaining in his room. It was a private party, just him and some cute little groupie." She shut her eyes to close out the memory, stiffening when Brian kissed her hair.

"What did you do?" he asked.

"I ran out to my car and drove back to school, angry and sad and hurt and confused. After the tournament P.J. showed up at my dorm and explained the differences between men and women. He talked about how men get lonely away from their families and how going to bed with a woman didn't mean he loved her like he loved my mother. He said my mother understood, and he hoped I would too."

Cuddling her as he would a child, Brian remained silent while shock, rage, and an agonizing sympathy raced through him. Fears weren't always rational, she'd said, but now he knew Pat's were.

Considering how she'd been hurt by her father and then how her husband had simply walked away from her, he felt despair turn his hot anger into solid ice. Loving Pat Langston, committing himself to a lifetime with her, would be the easy part for him. Convincing her he was worthy of her love would be a lot tougher.

Stroking her hair, he whispered, "I swear to you I'll never hurt you that way, Pat. I've never been to bed with a groupie, I've never even been tempted. If you believe nothing else of me, please believe that." The sad little shake of her head wrenched his heart, but he forced her head up, promising her with his eyes as well as his words.

"Sooner or later," she choked out through trembling lips, "you'll be tempted. And you'll give in."

He'd been expecting it, but it still hurt. Looking into her tear-filled eyes, Brian steadied her with a tender kiss. "Don't make me pay for your father's mistakes," he pleaded. "Don't make us both pay for his weakness." When she squeezed her eyes shut, he lightly thumbed her cheeks. "Give me—give us—a chance."

And when she opened her mouth to argue, he gave her something better to do.

The next afternoon, as he drove to the marina to pick up Pat, Brian vowed she'd never know what that day had cost him. He'd pluck every hair from his head before he'd let her know how tough it had been to watch her trot up to Seth Henderson that morning while he, Brian, stayed in the vehicle—at her request. And he'd give up fishing forever before he'd confess to spending the past eight hours watching the clock.

Remembering the pleasure he'd felt when he'd awakened that morning with Pat in his arms, he gripped the steering wheel more tightly. Delivering her to Seth Henderson this morning had been the first step toward proving that he could handle the demands of her career. Next weekend he'd take another step and impress her with his parental and housekeeping skills.

Slowing as he turned into the marina complex, Brian was surprised to see Henderson's bass rig loaded on the trailer at the side of the parking lot. He'd figured the kid would keep Pat out on the lake until the last possible minute.

Pulling into a spot some thirty feet from Henderson's rig, Brian fidgeted in his seat after turning off the motor, uncertain what to do. Pat had been adamant about his keeping a low profile that morning, but it'd sure be easier to wait if she weren't leaned over the boat, her head out of sight and her wet fanny aimed right at him.

Wet fanny?

With his temper rising faster than a rocket, Brian shoved open the door and jogged toward her, drawing in a sharp breath when Pat turned to face him. She was soaking wet! From her head to her toes.

"What the *hell*?" He made a beeline for Henderson.

"Brian!" When he hesitated at the sound of his name, Pat placed herself in front of him, her face as furious as her voice. "Stop right there," she ordered when he started toward Seth again.

Glaring at the younger man, Brian let her hand on his chest hold him still, but his fists remained clenched at his sides. "What did he do?" he bit out, a murderous glint in the gaze he kept on Seth.

Clamping down on the urge to tell Brian that

whatever had happened between her and Seth was none of his business, Pat tried to inject sanity into the situation. "Seth didn't *do* anything. We went catfish grappling, and I slipped and fell in a couple of times."

Turning an incredulous look on her, Brian backed up a step. "You did *what*?"

Pat plopped her hands on her hips, relieved that he'd backed off, but angry to the point of tears. "After we'd caught some bass, we left here and went catfish grappling up at Watts Bar Lake. It's something I've always wanted to do, and Seth offered to take me. I don't just write about bass fishing, Brian, and there's more to the outdoors than tournaments and fancy rigs."

"We got talking about things we'd always wanted—"

"*You* keep quiet," Brian ordered, jabbing a finger in Henderson's direction. "I am talking to Pat."

"No, you aren't," she countered, her voice rising several notes. "You're busy being an 'offended male,' jumping to conclusions and thinking the worst. And that's something I don't need, Brian." Turning to Seth, she stuck out her hand. "Thanks again for two great stories, and please accept my apology for this little scene."

Brian sulked. "You don't need to apologize for me."

"*Somebody* needs to apologize for you," she assured him. After one more scathing look, she stomped to the Blazer, her sneakers squishing with every step.

Shamed by Pat's last heated look, Brian watched her go, conscious of the smirk on Henderson's face. "I, um, I'm sorry. I guess I was . . . out of line," he stammered, wincing when Pat slammed the door on the Blazer with enough force to rock the vehicle.

"S'okay, man. I'd probably do the same thing if some guy brought my woman home looking like that."

His anger fading with the reasonableness of Seth's reply, Brian smiled. *His woman?* Dear Lord, he hoped Pat never heard anyone call her that.

Facing the younger man, he chuckled. "You really went catfish grappling?"

"Yeah. Got the fish and the scratches to show for it." Seth held out his arms, showing off scrapes on the backs of his hands. "Pat caught the biggest one. Want to see it?"

Glancing at the Blazer, Brian decided to give "his woman" a few more minutes to cool down. "She really did that? Groped under rocks for catfish? Barehanded?"

"The word is *grapple*, not *grope*. But don't ask me, ask him," Seth replied, holding up a fat-bellied catfish. Dropping the bewhiskered creature back into the livewell, he ducked his head, looking up at Brian through blond lashes. "That's some lady, there. I put my name on her dance card, in case you screw up."

Wincing at the younger man's crude phrasing, Brian shook hands with him again before heading for the Blazer with the enthusiasm of a rabbit rounding up a rattlesnake. He drew in a deep breath, bracing himself for Pat's fury, but when he eased open the door, the sound of sniffling wrenched his heart.

"Awww, baby, I'm sorry," he crooned, sliding onto the seat. He grimaced when she jerked away from his touch.

"I'm not your baby! How could you do that to me? I've never been so humiliated in my entire life."

Searching for the right words, he focused on what he'd like to do to himself at that moment. "Hit me."

Pat's eyes grew to huge proportions before she turned to look out the window. "Don't be ridiculous."

"I mean it, hit me," he repeated, balling one of her hands into a fist. "Like this." Tugging her hand to his chin, Brian made gentle contact. "But harder." He jutted his jaw, presenting a target she couldn't miss.

"I'm not going to hit you," she muttered to the window.

"It would make us both feel better."

This time she didn't even bother to speak to the pane of glass reflecting her misery.

"Okay, so it would make me feel better," Brian confessed, caught in a vacuum of frustration created by his own stupidity. "Come on, take a shot at it."

After listening to his own heart pounding for several moments, he sighed. "If you're not going to hit me, how about yelling at me? Tell me I made an ass of myself. Again."

"I told you it wouldn't work, Brian. *We* won't work."

Even knowing it was coming, he'd been unprepared for the depth of loss in Pat's voice. Despair settled like a solid chunk of lead in his gut when he realized the extent of the problem created by his desire to take care of "his woman."

Pat was writing him off, giving up on him. On them.

NINE

Pat divided her time the next Friday morning between packing, drilling the kids on emergency routines, and pacing her living-room floor. *How had she let Brian talk her into this?* He'd already proven he couldn't control his jealousy. What made him, or her, think he'd be able to change? And what kind of mother was she anyway, leaving her kids with a man they'd known less than a month?

"Damn," she muttered when the doorbell rang a few minutes before the man in question was scheduled to arrive. Steeling herself with the knowledge that this weekend would settle things for once and for all, she opened the door, prepared to fend off a passionate embrace.

She needn't have worried. Clutching grocery

bags in each arm, Brian merely kissed the air in her direction as he shoved past her. When she followed him to the kitchen, she eyed the brown array on her table in disbelief.

"You didn't have to bring food," she pointed out when he shooed her from the room. "I told you I'd stock the refrigerator with plenty of sandwich stuff. I assure you, the kids can survive a few days on pizza and bologna."

"Hush, woman," he scolded, brushing his lips over hers with a familiarity that made her gasp in exasperation. "I merely brought along what I need to cook my specialties."

"Your specialties?" Standing on tiptoe, she tried in vain to see over his shoulder, her curiosity spurred by Leslie's "oooh's" and "ahhh's."

"You know, fried chicken and stuff like that." Proving his reflexes were still in tip-top shape, Brian countered her attempts to peek into the kitchen.

Since he'd agreed to let her do the bulk of the cooking at the lake and had contented himself with manning the grill, she'd assumed he wasn't overly familiar with frying pans. "Fried chicken? You?"

"Uh-huh," he answered with a smug smile. "Yours will be the best-fed kids in Atlanta this weekend, so don't you worry your pretty head about them. Poppa Brian's got it all under control." Turning her around, he gave her a little shove. "Now, finish packing. You don't want to miss the cocktail party this evening."

She might as well have missed the cocktail party, Pat decided when she lifted the phone to call home some seven hours later. She barely remembered the three-hour drive to Augusta, and her mind had been in Atlanta all evening. Friends she hadn't seen in months had gradually drifted away when she failed to encourage their conversation.

When Scott answered the phone, she breathed a sigh of relief. At least one of her brood was alive and coherent.

"Everything okay?" she chirped, pretending a lightheartedness she didn't feel.

"Uhhh, yes, Mom," he answered. "Everything's great, just great. You want to talk to Brian?"

"In a minute." Her curiosity had been eating holes in her since Brian had carried in all those bags. "Did you have a good supper?"

"Yeah. We had fried chicken, and it was almost as good as yours. And we had mashed potatoes and biscuits and gravy."

"Everybody's okay, then?"

"We keep trying to tell you we're old enough to stay by ourselves."

Panic raced through her as she envisioned an adultless house. "Brian's not there?"

"He's here, playing Nintendo with Leslie, and she's beating the pants off him. I'll get him for you."

Releasing a breath she hadn't known she was holding, Pat waited, unprepared for the absurd joy that shot through her when Brian's soft drawl sounded in her ear. "Everything okay?" she asked, accepting that it would be her theme song for the weekend.

"Sure, we're doing fine. How about you? Having a good time?"

"Oh, yes. Wonderful. Fantastic," she blurted. "Tonight I got to visit with a lot of people I haven't seen in a while."

"Good. Missing you is easier if we know you're enjoying yourself."

"We?"

"The kids and me." The way he said it wrapped her in warmth. "That's a little philosophy Dusty shared with me tonight. He's really got his head on straight, you know. You should be proud of him."

"I'm proud of all my kids," she stated automatically. After several seconds she cleared her throat, knowing Brian was waiting for her to ask mommy-type questions. Determined to foil him, she managed a bright tone. "I'm in Room One-oh-two and you've got the motel number, right?"

"Let's see." Hearing paper rustling, she pictured him flipping through the notes she'd left. "I've got the motel number, your mother's number, both of your sisters' numbers, four of your neighbors' numbers, and of course Michael's number, down here at the bottom. And I've got your doctor's number and the pharmacy's number. Since I know how to dial nine-one-one, I think you covered all the bases, so stop worrying about us and have a good time."

Pat assured him she was having a good time.

After the first workshop the next day she hurried to her room and called home, but she hung up after the first ring, vowing to wait and call at her normal time in the evening. Despite her intentions, she tried again during the afternoon break, counting the rings until her answering machine picked up. She hung up without leaving a message.

At the banquet that evening the elderly lady sitting next to Pat leaned over and asked if she was ill. She'd barely touched her food, the woman pointed out, and in general didn't seem to be having a good time.

"I'm having a *wonderful* time," Pat insisted, smiling sweetly to prove her point. "I can't remember the last time I've had so much fun."

That night Dusty answered the phone, his voice making her feel a startling homesickness. Everything was fine, he assured her. They'd had ham and potato salad and cole slaw for supper.

"And peach cobbler, Mom. Boy, was it good," he added with blatant enthusiasm. "Leslie wrote down Brian's recipe for you." In the background she could hear Leslie and Scott laughing about something.

"How's Grady doing?" she asked with forced cheer.

"Umm, he's okay. Here's Brian."

"Hi, sweet lady," Brian said moments later. "I'm fine, the kids are fine, the house is fine, and the dog is fine."

"We don't have a dog. Do we?" she added hastily.

"Not that I know of." Brian's chuckle heated her blood. "I was just trying to put your mind at ease, everything's hunky-dory. How'd it go today?"

"How'd what go?"

"The meeting."

"Oh, the meeting. It was great. Wonderful. I learned a lot." In truth she couldn't remember a thing she'd heard. "A real nice lady sat next to me at the ban—what was that?"

"What was what?"

"That noise. It sounded like glass breaking."

There was the muted sound of a hand covering the mouthpiece, followed by the rumble of Brian's voice saying something she didn't quite catch. "I know you're tired," he suggested when he came back on the line seconds later, "and you've got a big day ahead of you tomorrow, so I guess I'd better let you go. Have a good time and drive very carefully. We'll be here when you get home."

"Brian? Are you sure—" She was talking to the dialtone. When she called home again seconds later, she got a busy signal.

Setting down the receiver, she told herself not to panic. Brian would have told her if there was anything wrong. *Unless he was in a hurry to call an ambulance.* She paced the floor for the next hour, stopping to send daggered looks at the telephone every few minutes.

After a sleepless night Pat was packed and ready to leave by six Sunday morning, but she forced herself to stay until after lunch. She'd promised to give Brian a chance to prove himself and, by golly, she was going to give him that chance, even if it caused her a nervous breakdown.

When she pulled onto her street a couple of hours ahead of schedule, the tight little fist that had been her stomach dropped to her toes. Brian's Blazer was not in her driveway. She cut off the engine before the car stopped rolling and hurried up the walkway.

When she flung open the front door and was greeted by the singular silence of an empty house, worry threatened to shut down her breathing process.

"Anybody home?" she called out, pushing away images of deadly havoc. Hearing no answer, she hurried through the living room, stopping at the foot of the stairs. "Hello? Where is everybody?"

A tomblike silence was her only answer.

Her gaze shot to the notepad by the phone, but there was no message. Forcing herself to take calming breaths, she trotted up the stairs, opening doors to check the kids' rooms as she went down the hall. They were all empty.

She paused outside her own room, her mind racing with possibilities. Maybe Brian had taken the kids to the mall. Maybe he'd forgotten to leave a note. Maybe they'd just gone to the corner store. Maybe they were hiding, planning to surprise her.

Rushing into the room before her imagination ran any wilder, she slumped with relief. Brian was there, on her bed, fast asleep. At least she thought he was asleep. Creeping closer, she drew in a shaky breath when she noted the steady rise and fall of his chest.

"Brian?" she whispered, unable to contain a smile when she bent over him. There was a heart-clutching vulnerability in his sprawled frame, and she doubted many people had ever caught Brian Culler napping.

Glancing around her room, she spotted nothing that belonged to him, not even his overnight bag. If he'd slept in here, as she'd planned, there was nothing to show of his presence, other than the gorgeous man himself. But of course she knew he was prone to neatness. He'd probably hung up his clothes and stored his bag in the closet. The thought of Brian's clothes hanging amid hers did strange things to her equilibrium, but she refused to let herself disprove her theory.

Brushing her lips over Brian's, she crooned, "Wake up, Sleeping Beauty."

His eyes popped open, exposing bloodshot whites. For a long moment he stared at her. Then he blinked, looked at the clock, smiled sleepily, and reached for her.

"You're home early," he mumbled, but when she accepted his kiss, he jerked away and shot off the bed, hobbling to the doorway. Leaning against the doorframe, he grinned. "The kids don't need to see us together in your bedroom."

Stunned by the comment, Pat opened her mouth, then closed it while she looked him over from head to toe.

"Why are you limping?" was her first question. "And what happened to your hand?"

She didn't miss the guilty look on his face when he tucked his bandaged right hand behind his back. Noting the puffy skin under his eyes, the sheer exhaustion on his face, Pat felt her stomach tighten again. "You look like hell, Brian. What's been going on? And what have you done with the kids? Where are they?"

He drew his left hand over his face as if he could erase the weariness there. "The kids are fine. Dusty and Scott went to the mall, they'll be home—"

"You let them go to the mall? In your Blazer?"

"They'd finished their chores, and Dusty's a good—"

"Chores?"

He nodded. "It didn't take long, with all of us pitching in."

Now that Pat thought about it, what she'd

seen of the house was cleaner than it had been in years. "Where's Leslie? And Grady?"

"Leslie's playing next door. She had a rough night, but—"

"What do you mean, a rough night?"

Brian shrugged again and shifted his weight, wincing when pain shot through his right ankle. Careful to keep the effort from his face, he sought a better position, finally settling for his original one, leaning on the doorframe. "She was sick and—"

"Sick? Why didn't you call me? What was wrong?"

"If you'll let me finish a sentence, I'll answer all your questions," he complained, tucking his right hand out of sight when he crossed his arms over his chest. When Pat mumbled a "sorry," he went on. "Leslie had an upset stomach. She probably ate too much junk food yesterday. She finally got it all out of her system about four this morning." He shook his head, still amazed by the resiliency of youth. "She was back to normal when she woke up later."

"You should have called me."

Her tone was an accusation, but Brian hadn't gone through all he'd gone through this weekend to give in now. "Not for an upset stomach. If it had been something serious, I would have called."

It was difficult to remain in the doorway while Pat wrestled with a multitude of emotions. It was even more difficult to refrain from comforting her when she slumped down onto the bed, but he didn't want Grady to find them in a position that could be considered compromising in any way. He'd had enough trouble with Grady, without that.

Brian had told Pat it would be fun getting to know each other, but he doubted she was finding this particular lesson fun. She'd obviously expected to return and discover him packed and ready to leave. She'd also obviously expected to find the house a wreck and the kids all wild and woolly after a weekend with the old bachelor.

"Come downstairs and I'll fill you in on the whole weekend," he coaxed, smiling when she rose and shuffled toward the door, her attitude one of helpless defeat. He knew her well enough to know she'd be back in form before long. Life with Patsy Jane McKinley Langston would never be dull, of that much he was sure.

His certainty was vindicated a moment later when Pat again asked why he was limping, her tone denying him an easy out. Even though she wasn't looking at him as she descended the stairs, he kept his face expressionless when he replied, "I twisted my ankle, playing volleyball with the boys."

She stopped and turned to look at him, her eyes filled with concern. "Is it serious? Did you go to the doctor?"

"No and no, it's just a slight sprain. It'll be good as new in a day or two." Grinning, he added, "I'm a poet, didja know it?"

Pat turned away with an unappreciative groan. Her next question was asked as she took another step down. "And your hand?"

Although he'd been expecting the question, Brian couldn't stop the involuntary grimace. "Nothing serious there, either, only a little burn."

She looked up at him from the bottom of the stairs, her eyes wide, glittering. "A burn? Brian, what on earth?"

Smiling with what he hoped she would perceive as male helplessness, he held out his hands. "I let the oil get a little too hot when I was frying chicken the other night." Moving past her, he finished his descent; the stairs were hell on his ankle.

He did his best to amble to the living room. "There was a little fire—"

"A fire!"

"—but nothing was damaged. Except my chicken," he corrected, gratefully sinking onto the sofa. "Grady put out the fire before it got out of the pan. I confess to letting the Colonel fix dinner after that."

Pat lowered herself to the sofa, too, disbelief plastered on her face. "A sick child, a sprained ankle, and a fire." Her head turned toward him with infinitesimal slowness. "Is there anything else you want to tell me?"

Meeting her worried gaze with as much confidence as he could muster, Brian bit down on the word no. He really didn't want to tell her the rest. "I'll put down new tile in your bathroom next week."

Pat burst to her feet. "New tile! In my bathroom!" Stomping to the window, she gripped the top of her head to keep it from blowing off. Her breathing was rapid as she counted to ten. And twenty. And thirty.

It didn't help.

Spinning toward Brian, she held up her hands in a futile gesture and shouted, "Why does my bathroom need new tile? It was fine when I left!"

"I'm afraid we had a little flood up there."

"*A little flood?* How could you have a flood in my bathroom?"

"I forgot to turn off the water to the house when I fixed your leaky faucet," he said, his tone reasonable. "Actually the floor's probably okay, but if it isn't, Grady's promised to help me fix it."

Collapsing in a heap on the sofa, she put out her hand when Brian started to scoot toward her. "Don't," she ordered in a soft voice, "just don't."

"I was going to—"

"I know what you were 'going to do.' "

"—hold you," he finished, his dark eyes pools of hurt.

"I know it sounds bad, Pat, but the weekend was actually pretty great. We all survived, didn't we? Isn't that what counts?"

"Please, be quiet," she begged, her mind grappling with the multidisasters he'd related in such a calm manner. "I need a few minutes. . . ." Wafting her hands through the air, she looked at him in mute dismay.

Grunting with the effort, Brian pushed himself up off the sofa. "I'll get my stuff together," he said, standing over her. When she refused to meet his gaze, he limped from the room.

Moments later he called out from upstairs, "Pat? Where's Grady?"

Still befuddled by all that had happened in her absence, she didn't answer right away. But when Brian's question penetrated the confusion in her mind, she jerked to her feet and bolted to the stairs. Brian was leaning against the banister at the top.

"Where's he supposed to be?" she asked, trying to keep the worry from her voice.

"In his room. He was on restriction."

"Oh, Lord." Pat groaned, taking the stairs two at a time. At the top she blew past Brian and raced into the twins' room, her heart thumping like a bass drum. "There's a note," she yelped, snatching the paper from the dresser.

Dear Mom, it read, *I'm going to live with Dad. I hope you and Brian will be very happy. Love, your son, Grady.*

Shoving the paper into Brian's hands she demanded, "What happened between you two? What did you do to him?"

He read the note before looking at her, his expression worried and defensive. "I didn't do anything to him, except put him on restriction for not doing his chores today."

"What were his chores?"

Shrugging, Brian handed the note back to her. "Take out the trash, sweep and mop the kitchen floor. Dusty said he—"

Pat waved away the rest of his explanation. "Nothing else happened between you two?"

"Nothing of any importance," Brian hedged. He'd lost now, anyway, no point in making things worse. Pat might have been able to handle the other stuff, once she'd had time to think about it, but no way would he ask her to trade her son for him.

Thinking back over the weekend, he asked himself what he should have done differently or if he could have done something more to win Grady over. For the life of him, he couldn't think of a thing. All in all, he thought he'd handled the problem well, despite Grady's attempts to create havoc. He had to give the boy credit, Grady had played his ace in the hole at the most critical moment. The kid had known all along how to keep his mom from getting involved with any man.

Refusing to let bitterness engulf him, Brian kept his misery from his voice when he spoke. "I'll help you straighten this out."

"You've helped enough, Brian."

The words ripped through him, slicing his last tiny thread of hope. "I'm sorry, Pat, I didn't think he disliked me this much," he offered, opening his arms to comfort her. When she turned her back to him, he lowered his hands. "I'll go pack and get out of your way."

Turning to leave, he struggled to breathe around the genuine helplessness ballooning within him.

Refusing to look at Brian again, Pat reached for the phone by her son's bed, noting the yellow pages directory opened to the listings of cab companies. Uncertain if her heartache was for Grady or herself, she punched out her ex-husband's phone number, bracing herself for his lecture.

She was listening to the third ring when a sound made her whirl toward the doorway. Loosing a small cry, she cradled the receiver and hurried to Grady, crushing her to him without thought of his usual protest.

"Thank God," she said, backing off to look at him.

"Oh, Mom, I'm sorry," Grady said, leaning into her again, his slender frame jerking with the effort to contain a sob. "Dad wasn't home, but I didn't really want to live with him anyway. Can I stay with you?"

The agony in his question made it hard for her to speak. "Of course you can stay with me. You're my son and I love you. You're one of the most important parts of my life, and I don't know what I'd do without you here."

"But what about Brian?" He pushed back to study her with watery gray eyes. He lowered his head to her shoulder again, oblivious of the man who now stood behind him. "He hates me."

Engulfed by the pain in Brian's eyes and the abject misery in her son's voice, Pat swallowed around the lump in her throat. "Why do you think Brian hates you?"

"Because I was so mean this weekend. I made him hurt his ankle and burn his hand and flood your bathroom." Grady again raised his head and sniffled. "But today I thought about how hard you've worked to take care of us and how lonely you probably get sometimes. I thought if I went to live with Dad, Brian would want to marry you. He likes Dusty and Scott and Leslie."

Helplessly Pat stared at the shimmering image of Brian, holding in a sob of her own when he reached out and put his hand on Grady's shoulder.

"I like you, too, son," he said, his voice hoarse with emotion. "I know you're scared and you're worried about your mom, but it's okay, we'll work it out." Pausing, he looked into Pat's eyes. "I do want to marry your mother," he went on, aiming his words at her as much as at Grady, "but it's a package deal. I get you all, or I get nothing."

Grady straightened and swiped a hand over his eyes. "You'd want me to live with you and Mom?"

"Sure. Every family needs a quick-thinking fireman," Brian joked, his chuckle dying in his throat when Grady fell against his chest. Blinking against tears, the National Bass Trail's current National Champ managed a quivery smile for Pat as he wrapped his arms around her son.

A half hour later Pat's heart jumped into her throat yet again when the kids said good-bye to Brian. It had been an emotional afternoon, and there were still things that needed to be said between them.

While Brian had gathered his gear, she'd listened to three slightly different and somewhat embellished versions of the weekend, each of which ended in the words "It was neat." Although Grady had remained silent for the most part, she'd sensed his regret over his actions.

"What exactly went on between you and Grady?" she asked Brian after the kids made obvious and enthusiastic excuses for disappearing.

Bending to pick up his overnight bag, he shook his head. "Nothing serious." When he straightened, he snapped his fingers as if he'd just remembered something. "Oh, yeah, the noise you heard last night? Scott and Leslie were horsing around and they accidentally broke a vase. I'll replace it for you."

"That's not necessary, Brian. I want to know about Grady. How'd you hurt your ankle?"

A reluctant sigh slipped from him. "I went up to block a high shot from Scott during our volleyball game. When I came down, I fell over Grady. He'd asked to be on my team."

Nodding, Pat prodded, "And your hand?"

"A minor burn," Brian assured her, holding up the bandaged hand with endearing nonchalance. "Leslie wanted me to watch her do a cartwheel, so I cut the heat down under the pan before I stepped out of the kitchen. When I returned, the eye was red-hot, and the pan burst into flames when I tried to move it. Grady was Johnny-on-the-spot with the extinguisher."

"I see." And she did, but she wanted to know the rest. "And I suppose Grady offered to turn off the water so you could fix my faucet?"

"You got it," Brian confirmed, "but don't be too hard on him, he's a little confused. He loves you and he's having a hard time accepting another man's presence in your life. Today was a real breakthrough for both of us."

She clamped down on the urge to ask how a diehard bachelor had gotten to be such an expert in child psychology, saying instead, "You could have been seriously hurt."

"But I wasn't," he pointed out with that

maddening reasonableness she'd come to love. Setting his bag on the floor again, Brian pulled her to him. "I think the weekend went well, all things considered."

"You certainly seem to be a big hit with the kids," she agreed.

"What about with their mom? Did I pass the test, Pat?"

She dipped her head, not wanting to see the need in his eyes. "With flying colors," she admitted somewhat miserably. Once again he'd foiled her plan to scare him off. "Of course, those colors are mostly black and blue."

Brian didn't laugh at her joke. If the love in his eyes hadn't stolen her breath, his next words would have. "I love you and I want to marry you. I know my being a longtime bachelor bothers you, but consider this: I've never before asked a woman to marry me. Doesn't that count for something?"

Turning her head, Pat kissed his palm, inhaling the wonderful scent of his skin. "I'm really honored," she whispered into his hand, "and I'd like to think it would work, but—"

"But I'm a professional fisherman," he finished for her, exasperation threaded through the words.

Frustrated by his failure to understand, she

slid her arms around him and molded her body to his, feeling his instant response. "Can't we just sort of see each other now and then?" she pleaded, moving seductively against him. "With both our travel schedules, that's about all we could expect if we were married."

Lowering his head, Brian kissed her with a tenderness that curled her toes, but when he pulled away, she knew she'd lost yet another battle.

"No, we can't just see each other now and then," he contended, stroking his fingers through her hair as he looked at her with hungry eyes. "I had a long talk with the twins this weekend about dating and sex—"

"What?" Pat pulled away in shock.

"—and I realized I couldn't preach one thing to them and practice another with you. So I'm not going to make love to you again until we're married."

She was flabbergasted. "What did you tell the boys?"

Rocking back on his heels, Brian shoved his hands in his pockets and grinned at her as he had the first night they'd met. "I told them they should treat the girls they date the way they would want someone to treat their sister. Thinking of Leslie as my almost-daughter has put a different perspective on things for me, and I was trying to share that perspective with the boys."

For the second time that afternoon Pat collapsed onto the sofa. It was too much. It was all too much.

"I've thought about the other problem," Brian went on, his voice a shade too casual, "and I've decided I can't help you with it. You'll have to find it in yourself to believe a man could love you so much, he'd never even look at another woman. Trust is an important part of love, Pat. Without it, we have nothing."

He went down on one knee, cradling her face in his hands so that she couldn't turn away from the promise in his dark eyes. "I swear to you, you can trust me. I'd rather cut out my heart than hurt you."

"But Brian, I—"

"Shhh. Don't say anything right now, it's been a tough afternoon." Rising to his feet, he planted a soft kiss on her forehead before limping to his bag.

Pat watched him hobble to the foyer. Torn between her common sense and her uncommon feelings, she called out, "Brian?"

When he turned to face her, she stood, but

she couldn't make herself go to him. "When will I see you again?"

The concern in his eyes belied the smile on his lips. "This weekend you trusted me with your kids," he gently pointed out. "Call me when you can trust me with your heart."

TEN

Brian impatiently scanned the room. He was caught in a classic "good news, bad news" situation. The good news was he was leading the field after the first day of fishing on Georgia's Lake Sidney Lanier. The bad news was he didn't give a damn.

After nearly three weeks with no word from Pat, he'd finally been forced to accept her refusal to let him into her life. It hurt like hell, but Brian understood how the betrayals in her past had stacked the deck against him. He also understood it was time to reorder his priorities, but how in the hell was he supposed to do that?

Glancing at the supple blonde gracing his right arm, he hoped he was making a move in the right direction.

"Congratulations, Brian, you had a great day."

"Thanks." He shook hands with Seth Henderson.

"A win here will anchor you in the number-one spot going into the National, won't it?" the young man asked, looking at the woman at Brian's side. The fact that she was at least fifteen years older than Henderson didn't keep the kid from visibly appreciating her curves.

Brian dipped his head and studied his sneakers, ignoring Seth's obvious desire for an introduction. He couldn't ignore Pat's influence, though. Raising his head, he gave the kid a halfhearted smile. "You're not far behind me on the leader board. You could slip up and win this one. That wouldn't be a bad way to end the year, would it?"

"It would be better to end the year at the National."

"There's always next year." Pain jabbed Brian as he remembered Pat speaking those exact words to him. It was ironic, he thought now, that he didn't even need to place in this tournament. He'd racked up enough points in the past couple of weeks to guarantee him an invitation to the National, two weeks away. A win here would simply put him at the top of the standings going in.

"Yeah, there's always next year," Henderson said, grinning with the enthusiasm of youth. "How much money did you win this year, Brian?"

He shook his head, determined to ignore the rudeness in the question. "Enough to make it worth my while, I suppose." Looking across the room, he spotted a familiar large frame. "If you'll excuse me, I've got some business to discuss with Bo," he said with brusque efficiency, moving past Henderson.

"Well, good luck tomorrow."

Surprised by the kid's words, Brian stopped and fixed him with a curious look.

"And good luck at the National," Seth added.

"Yeah, thanks," was all he could manage to say. Shaking his head, he watched Henderson walk away. Maybe the kid was growing up.

"Why didn't you introduce me?" the dark-eyed woman beside Brian asked.

Meeting the innocence in her eyes, he shook his head. "Maybe later. Right now, there's someone else I need to catch," he explained, urging her toward Bo. As she hurried along beside him, Brian was conscious of her gaze on his face.

After introducing his companion to Simpson, Brian tamped down a crazy kind of jealousy when they lingered over pleasantries.

"Seen Pat lately?" he asked when silence descended between them.

Simpson's baby blues twinkled with unspoken questions. "Nope. I was about to ask if you'd seen her. I take it you two had some problems?"

"You take it right."

"That's a shame, Bubba, a real shame. Can I do anything to help?"

"As a matter of fact you probably can. I need to talk with you about something, if you can spare me a few minutes."

Bo looked at the woman clinging to Brian, then back to the Champ. "You want to go to my room? We can talk there."

"Why don't we all go to the lounge?" Brian's blond companion asked. "I'd like a drink, and Brian could sure use some cheering up. I've been trying all evening to get a smile out of him."

When Bo still hesitated, she granted him a dazzling smile. "We won't stay long. I'm a little tired from the drive here today, and Brian and I have to get to bed early tonight."

When Pat pulled her car into the motel parking lot, she left the engine running for a long time while she convinced herself all over again she was doing the right thing. Since she'd last seen Brian, she'd come to believe he loved her, but she was still afraid to trust him.

Not him, his career, she corrected herself as she turned off the engine. Staring out at the dark expanse that was Lake Sidney Lanier, she bolstered her courage with the memory of the Champ down on one knee telling her he'd rather cut out his heart than hurt her.

After three weeks of living hell made worse by writing about Brian every day, she'd finally finished the book copy. And she'd also conceded that she'd never be happy unless she gave Brian Culler the benefit of the doubt. If things didn't work out, if he gave in to the temptations of the road . . .

Pat didn't want to think about the painful consequences she might face one day. For now she had to love Brian with everything that was in her. She had no choice in the matter, her life felt empty without him.

She pushed away all negative thoughts and pictured instead Brian's delight when he saw her tonight. As she headed for the motel, she felt a surge of joy.

In her haste to find the man she loved, she caught her pocketbook on the lobby door, and when she turned to free it, Bo Simpson's voice drifted to her. Whirling toward the sound, she felt her heart slide to her toes in a frozen lump as Bo's name died on her lips, but it wasn't her big friend who filled her with panic. There was no mistaking the lean frame spotlighted in the lounge doorway some thirty feet away. There was also no mistaking the adoration on the face of the blond woman who was hanging on to Brian as if her life depended on melding her flesh with his.

Choking back a cry, Pat jerked her purse free and fled from the lobby. In her car she shoved the keys into the ignition before she broke down and sobbed, beating her fist against the steering wheel every few minutes. Her anger was aimed at herself more than at Brian.

"Fool!" She pounded the wheel. "Stupid, stupid fool!" Try as she might, she couldn't push away the image of her father in bed with a woman who wasn't his wife. *"Trust me,"* she mouthed sarcastically, squeezing her eyes shut against a similar image of Brian, his dark head sharing a pillow with a blond one.

It took a while to get it all out of her system, but when she finished, Pat felt cleansed and in control again. Leaning back against the headrest, she cruelly replayed the picture of Brian Culler entering the smoky lounge with a slinky blonde on his arm. So he'd never been tempted by groupies? She understood it now.

He'd shot straight past temptation on his way to participation.

Remembering Bo, Pat clutched her stomach, groaning in misery. Brian's betrayal was almost more than she could bear, but in time she'd get over it. She might never get over her best friend's treachery. Bo was the one who'd first realized she was in love with Brian, so how could he sit back and watch while Brian screwed around?

"Sit back and watch?" she muttered out loud. "He was tagging along like a lovesick puppy. Probably hoping for Brian's leavings." Putting her fist to her mouth, she fought down yet another sob. "You'll pay for this, Brian Culler!" A plan formed as she stared out across the dark lake. Smiling with bitter pleasure, she started her car and pulled out of the parking lot.

A half hour later she pulled back in, her heart pounding with the hope that she wasn't too late. Picturing the scene a tardy arrival would cause, she decided it didn't matter. Either way, Brian Culler would be taught a lesson.

Grabbing the pink bag from the seat beside her, she rushed to the lobby again, smiling around her embarrassment when the clerk eyed her warily.

"Hi, I'm Mrs. Brian Culler," she cooed, leaning over the counter to give the young man a view of her less than spectacular cleavage. "I seem to have lost the key to our room, and my husband's out with the boys. Could you please let me in?"

"Do you have any identification, Mrs. Culler?"

"Oh, dear, we're on our honeymoon," she crooned, digging in the bag. "I haven't changed my name on my ID yet." Pulling out a skimpy black negligee, she held it up, making sure he saw the tag hanging from it. "I just went to town to get this." That much was the truth, at least. "And I must have left the key in the room. I did *so* want to surprise him when he got back. Can't you help me do something nice for my brand-new husband?" Pouting, she held up a twenty-dollar bill. "I'd be *so* grateful to you."

Five minutes later she fell onto the bed in Brian's room in a heap of hilarity. She allowed herself to stay there only a moment, though. She wanted everything to be ready for his return.

"Talk about catching a man with his pants down," she muttered. "From now on, he'll think twice before he takes a woman to his room." The laugh that slipped from her was one she usually stored with her Halloween costume.

After strategically placing her shoes, hose, blouse, skirt, slip, bra, and panties along what appeared to be a haphazard path to the bed,

Pat draped the lacy black negligee over the lampshade. When the suggestive composition met with her approval, she slid between the sheets and twisted onto her stomach. With deliberate care, she arranged the top sheet so it covered only her buttocks and one leg, then bent the exposed leg at the knee in what she hoped was a sensuous pose. After mussing her hair and trying out several arm positions, she settled in to wait. She was in no danger of going to sleep.

Some twenty minutes later the sound of a key in the lock sent panic shooting through her. The door opened. Sickeningly feminine laughter bubbled around words Brian spoke.

"Oh, Brian, I'm so excited," the woman positively burbled. "I can't wait to get started."

Taking that as her cue, Pat raised her head and looked at the pair. "Is that you, Brian?" she mumbled, feigning heavy eyelids and unfocused vision. "What took you so long?" she scolded through pouted lips. "I've been so lonely without you. Come over here and give me a kiss."

The woman's shocked gasp was all Pat could ask for, but the glint in Brian's eyes was another thing altogether.

Without a word he removed the blonde's hand

from his arm and left her staring in amazement while he strode to the bed and bent to kiss Pat. When she rolled to get away, he came heavily down on top of her, pinning her in place as he plundered her mouth with a force that made her cry out.

"Oh, God, I'm sorry," he said. "I didn't mean to hurt you, but—" Whatever else he was going to say was cut off by another hungry kiss. And another and another. It was quite a dizzying experience, Pat discovered.

And quite embarrassing.

"Brian!" she yelped when he released her mouth. "Stop it!" Ignoring her, he lowered his head again. Several more seconds passed before she could break free.

"Ooooohhhhh, you two-timing son of a—" His mouth covered hers again. "Get off me, you lying—" was all she managed before he claimed her lips once more, drawing a shameless reaction from her. Frustrated by her body's betrayal, she twisted her head away from Brian and pushed against his shoulders. When he forced her head back toward him, she squealed in frustration. It didn't stop him from kissing her.

"You'd do it, wouldn't you?" she seethed when he came up for air. "You'd really do it?"

"Do what?" he feinted toward her left ear

and planted a kiss on her right temple when she countered the move.

"Have sex with me with . . . with"—she dodged an attempt aimed at her mouth—"*her* here."

"Her who?" His hands began a slow slide up her ribs.

"Her!" Capturing his hands, Pat jabbed a nod in the woman's direction.

"Oh, her," Brian said, grinning before he claimed her lips again. "She won't mind waiting," he suggested when next he raised his head.

It was Pat's turn to gasp. Narrowing her eyes, she threatened, "I'll scream, Brian, I swear I will."

"I'm planning on it," he returned, chuckling when another furious growl slipped from her mouth into his. This time he kissed her with a thoroughness that melted her speech center.

Satisfied he'd quieted her, Brian relinquished her lips, his eyes twinkling with amusement now. "Of course, if Marilyn makes you nervous, I'll ask her to leave." Glancing over his shoulder, he smiled at the other woman. "Looks like we're going to be busy for a while. Will you excuse us, hon?"

"I don't believe you!" Pat was furious with herself; she squirmed like a worm on a hook. That only made things worse, she discovered.

"You'd better believe him, honey." This came from the other woman. "He's probably not going to let you out of his sight again."

"She's right," Brian agreed, nodding with serious intent. "I'm not letting you out of my sight until you're wearing my ring. If that means I have to keep you naked and in bed, so be it."

"Dammit, Brian! Who *is* she?" Pushing against his chest, Pat stared at the lithe blonde, noting for the first time the familiar shape of the slightly squared chin.

"My name's Marilyn Hodge, honey. I'm Brian's sister," the woman said, strolling to the door with unselfconscious grace. "And I'm real glad you finally came to your senses. Now maybe my little brother will smile again. He's been a real bear these past few weeks."

With one mighty shove Pat dumped Brian onto the floor. Snatching the sheet to her chest, she glared at him. "Your sister? She's your sister?"

"She also happens to be Carrie and Travis's mother," he offered with a lecherous grin.

"Pleased to meet you," Marilyn said, her dark eyes gleaming with amusement as she opened the door. "My kids have told me a lot about you, almost as much as Brian has. Now I guess I've got something to tell them." She winked. " 'Night, little brother. See you in the morning."

She snagged the DO NOT DISTURB sign and looped it over the outside knob. "Then again, maybe I won't." She closed the door.

Kneeling by the bed, Brian reached for Pat again, laughing when she indignantly scooted away.

"I want to know what's going on, Brian," she demanded. "Why is your sister here?"

Tugging off his shoes, he shrugged. "I told you, she's had it rough since Sammy's death." He stood and placed his sneakers next to Pat's flimsy sandals, then shucked off his socks and placed them next to her hose. "She's going to help manage my tackle company. I thought this would be a good place to get her talking to some of the guys about repping for us." Casting a look of measured caution at Pat, he added, "I think Bo likes her."

Pat didn't care if Bo liked Brian's sister or not. "You have a tackle company?"

Reaching for the top button on his shirt, Brian pinned her in place with a look of pure need. "Not yet, but I will in a few months. I'm retiring from the circuit after the National."

Unable to tear her gaze from the chest he was steadily exposing, Pat said, "You're kidding! Why would you do that?"

He paused to consider the array of clothing

on the floor, then dropped his shirt next to hers. "So maybe a certain 'Fishermom' will trust me enough to marry me."

"Oh, Brian." She moaned. "You don't have to do that." When he shrugged off her protest, she went weak with love. "You're going to be the first three-time National Champ."

"I'd rather be your husband," he said simply, sliding his belt from his jeans. After a moment of contemplation, he put it next to her slip.

Watching him unsnap his pants, Pat blinked back tears. "Maybe you can be both."

His hands stilled on his zipper. "What did you say?"

Meeting the question in his eyes with love in hers, she smiled. "I said, maybe you can be both. If you can win two more championships, that is." Her smile widened when she saw joy sparkle in his.

Pulling off his jeans, Brian balanced on one foot, then the other. Without looking, he deposited the crisp denim next to Pat's skirt. Hooking his thumbs into the top of his briefs, he hesitated, drawing his brows together as if he'd discovered a new concern.

"Why are you here, Pat?"

Letting her eyes absorb his very special

beauty, she laughed. "Isn't it obvious? I crave your body."

He shook his head, his expression serious and eyes searching hers. "Don't joke with me right now, sweet lady. Why are you here?"

Pat swallowed hard, not certain she could say what he wanted to hear. Concentrating on the depth of love shining in his dark eyes, she drew in one deep breath and let it out. "I'm here because I love you and I want to spend the rest of my life with you. Starting tonight."

He went very still then, as if he'd forgotten how to breathe, and in that stillness Pat sensed an eternal commitment. Several long moments passed before she could find voice enough to speak.

"I thought we weren't going to make love again until after we were married," she teased lightly, aware her voice sounded loud in the quiet of the room. "What happened to 'practicing what you preach'?"

Brian blinked as if he were awaking from a dream. "As far as I'm concerned," he said, his tone leaving her no doubt he was serious, "we got married when you crawled into my bed tonight. We'll take care of the legalities tomorrow." Stripping off the briefs, he flashed his charmer grin. "Any more questions, Mrs. Patsy Jane McKinley Langston Culler?"

"There is one more thing—I thought you needed to get to sleep early tonight. Have you forgotten your five-thirty appointment at the marina in the morning?"

"I've forgotten everything except how much I love you," he assured her, snatching away the sheet.

But when an aggravating buzz pulled him from a deep sleep a few hours later, Brian realized he'd forgotten one other thing—to turn off his alarm. Groggily he reached for the noisemaker, smiling when Pat shifted against him. As he lay there in the dark, cuddling her to him, he breathed in the first total contentment he'd ever known.

"Get up, sleepyhead," Pat mumbled, pushing him away. "You've got a tournament to win."

"Huh-unh, I've got a marriage license to buy," he argued. "I don't want you running away from me."

"I'm not going anywhere." Sitting up, she switched on the light, grinning when he groaned a complaint. "Trust is an important part of love, Brian. Without it, we have nothing."

Squinting against the brightness, he reached for her. "Okay, we don't have to get the license today. But I could stay here and practice for our honeymoon." His attempt to kiss her netted him a mouthful of pillow.

"Well, if you're not going to make wild, crazy love with me," he grumbled, "I guess I might as well go fishing."

EPILOGUE

Rolling onto her side, Pat reached across the bed, groaning when she realized she was alone. Through sleep-fogged eyes she scanned the room, seeking Brian.

Groaning again, she stretched listlessly, trying to dredge up enough strength to drag herself from the bed. She felt so satiated. How could Brian have the energy to move, much less the ability to leave their bed, after the long loving they'd shared?

She captured a yawn behind her hand, knowing she was feeling the effects of more than luxurious lovemaking. It had been a long day driving home from the National with all the kids in the new van.

Slipping from the bed, Pat pulled on her robe

and padded from the room, making her way unerringly to the small bedroom in the opposite wing of the house. Leslie and Scott had upstairs bedrooms, and the twins, now in their first year at Chattanooga's East Tennessee University, had claimed the boat-house apartment a few months earlier.

"Something wrong?" she whispered, going down on her knees by the rocking chair Brian had handcrafted for her.

"No, nothing's wrong," he whispered in reply, his lopsided grin flashing at her in the dim light from the window. "In fact I'd say everything's right."

Resting her head on his knee, Pat relished the feeling of total contentment in knowing he was there, with her. Times like these made up for all the nights they couldn't be together.

She was quiet for several moments before asking, "How does it feel, Mr. Three-Time Champ?"

There was a short silence while he considered the question. "It feels great, but not as great as being home."

Brian sighed, wondering how the fatigue of the past few days could just dissolve when he walked in the door of this house. It never failed to surprise him. He'd be worn out from a tournament, weary from the road, and then he'd pull into the driveway, walk through the front door, and be renewed by this woman. By his family.

"When are you leaving for Kentucky?" He knew she was supposed to go at the end of the week, but he also knew Pat sometimes delayed her departure until the absolute last minute. They certainly had that much in common—both of them hated leaving home these days.

He smiled. They had a great many things in common, and soon they'd have even more. They were coauthoring a book on fishing. His smile widened. It wouldn't take long for Pat Langston's fans to realize her husband was riding her coattails on this project. .

Thinking about the question, Pat grinned. In the future she would be traveling less and concentrating her efforts on writing fiction. She'd also be working more closely with Marilyn, helping promote the new tackle company that was casting its reps into the winner's circle with regularity.

"I'd planned to leave Friday afternoon," she drawled, "but if I get up really early, I can wait until Saturday morning." She would be gone three days—three long, lonely days.

The time away from home was tolerable only because she felt so loved, so secure and happy. And because she knew Brian would take care of things in her absence. In the past twelve months he'd more than proven himself to be totally capable and undeniably trustworthy. Not only had he achieved his professional goal, he'd negotiated the treacherous waters of instant fatherhood with admirable skill. While it hadn't been all smooth sailing, it also hadn't been as stormy as Pat had feared it would be.

"You hate to get up early," Brian reminded her, pulling her thoughts back to her upcoming trip.

She chuckled. "But I hate sleeping without you even more."

Stroking his hand over her hair, Brian nodded. "I hate for you to sleep without me too." Without warning, tears formed in his eyes. "Thank you," he whispered.

"Brian Culler, what are you thanking me for now?"

"For being you. For being here. For loving me." Cupping her chin, he let her see the emotion in his eyes. "For giving me this wonderful, precious gift."

Moving his hand from her face to his son's back, he carefully lowered the baby from his shoulder to his lap, gazing into the little face with heartfelt wonder. Of all the things Pat had added to his life, this was the absolute best.

Looking at the child, he shook his head, remembering Pat's words on the night they were officially married.

"When I decide to do something, I do it," she'd said, the imp in her eyes dancing. "I've decided I want to have babies with you, and since I'm not getting any younger, I suggest we get started pretty soon."

Clearing his throat, Brian struggled to speak around the emotions welling in him. "Everybody's wondering what we'll do at next year's National. We're a major attraction now, after getting married there last year and showing off the baby this year. Got any ideas?"

Smiling in the manner that always heated his blood, Pat rose and kissed him lightly on the lips. "If you'll tuck this little bundle of joy back into his crib," she whispered, bending to kiss her sleeping son's face, "we can go to our room and work on my idea. I think this little guy could use another sister, don't you?"

Easing to his feet, Brian cradled his son against him a few seconds longer before settling the baby in his crib. Reluctant to leave the miracle Pat had given him, he smiled down at "Little Brian," as the child had been dubbed by Bo.

"Bri . . . an." Pat leaned against the doorframe, waiting for him.

"Another sister, huh?" he asked, chuckling as he considered the idea. Before she could say anything, he scooped up his wife and claimed the perfection of her lips, demonstrating his enthusiasm for her new project.

THE EDITOR'S CORNER

There's never too much of a good thing when it comes to romances inspired by beloved stories, so next month we present TREASURED TALES II. Coming your way are six brand-new LOVESWEPTs written by some of the most talented authors of romantic fiction today. You'll delight in their contemporary versions of age-old classics . . . and experience the excitement and passion of falling in love. TREASURED TALES II— what a way to begin the new year!

The first book in our fabulous line up is **PERFECT DOUBLE** by Cindy Gerard, LOVESWEPT #660. In this wonderful retelling of *The Prince and the Pauper* business mogul Logan Prince gets saved by a stranger from a near-fatal mugging, then wakes up in an unfamiliar bed to find a reluctant angel with a siren's body bandaging his wounds! Logan vows to win Carmen Sanchez's heart—

even if it means making a daring bargain with his look-alike rescuer and trading places with the cowboy drifter. It take plenty of wooing before Carmen surrenders to desire—and even more sweet persuasion to regain her trust once he confesses to his charade. A top-notch story from talented Cindy.

Homer's epic poem *The Odyssey* has never been as romantic as Billie Green's version, **BABY, COME BACK**, LOVESWEPT #661. Like Odysseus, David Moore has spent a long time away from home. Finally free after six years in captivity, and with an unrecognizable face and voice, he's not sure if there's still room for him in the lives of his sweet wife, Kathy, and their son, Ben. When he returns home, he masquerades as a handyman, determined to be close to his son, aching to show his wife that, though she's now a successful businesswoman, she still needs him. Poignant and passionate, this love story shows Billie at her finest!

Tom Falconson lives the nightmare of *The Invisible Man* in Terry Lawrence's **THE SHADOW LOVER**, LOVESWEPT #662. When a government experiment goes awry and renders the dashingly virile intelligence agent invisible, Tom knows he has only one person to turn to. Delighted by mysteries, ever in search of the unexplained, Alice Willow opens her door to him, offering him refuge and the sensual freedom to pull her dangerously close. But even as Tom sets out to show her that the phantom in her arms is a flesh-and-blood man, he wonders if their love is strong enough to prove that nothing is impossible. Terry provides plenty of thrills and tempestuous emotions in this fabulous tale.

In Jan Hudson's **FLY WITH ME**, LOVESWEPT #663, Sawyer Hayes is a modern-day Peter Pan who soars through the air in a gleaming helicopter. He touches down in Pip LeBaron's backyard with an offer of a job in his company, but the computer genius quickly informs him that for now she's doing nothing except making up for the childhood she missed. Bewitched by her delicate beauty, Sawyer decides to help her, though her kissable mouth persuades him that a few grown-up games would be more fun. Pip soon welcomes his tantalizing embrace, turning to liquid moonlight beneath his touch. But is there a future together for a man who seems to live for fun and a lady whose work has been her whole life? Jan weaves her magic in this enchanting romance.

"The Ugly Duckling" was Linda Cajio's inspiration for her new LOVESWEPT, **HE'S SO SHY**, #664—and if there ever was an ugly duckling, Richard Creighton was it. Once a skinny nerd with glasses, he's now impossibly sexy, irresistibly gorgeous, and the hottest actor on the big screen. Penelope Marsh can't believe that this leading man in her cousin's movie is the same person she went to grade school with. She thinks he's definitely out of her league, but Richard doesn't agree. Drawn to the willowy schoolteacher, Richard dares her to accept what's written in the stars—that she's destined to be his leading lady for life. Linda delivers a surefire hit.

Last, but certainly not least, is **ANIMAL MAGNETISM** by Bonnie Pega, LOVESWEPT #665. Only Dr. Dolittle is Sebastian Kent's equal when it comes to relating to animals—but Danni Sullivan insists the veterinarian still needs her help. After all, he's new in her hometown, and no one knows every cat, bull, and pig there as well as she. For once giving in to impulse, Sebastian hires her on the spot—then thinks twice about it when her touch arouses long-denied yearnings. He can charm any beast, but he definitely needs a lesson in how to soothe his wounded heart. And Danni has just the right touch to heal his pain—and make him believe in love once more. Bonnie will delight you with this thoroughly enchanting story.

Happy reading!

With warmest wishes,

Nita Taublib

Nita Taublib

Associate Publisher

P.S. Don't miss the fabulous women's fiction Bantam has coming in January: **DESIRE**, the newest novel from bestselling author Amanda Quick; **LONG TIME COMING,** Sandra Brown's classic contemporary romance; **STRANGER IN MY ARMS** by R. J. Kaiser, a novel of romantic suspense in which a woman who has lost her memory is in danger of also losing her life; and **WHERE DOLPHINS GO** by LOVESWEPT author Peggy Webb, a truly unique romance that integrates into its story the fascinating ability of dolphins to aid injured children. We'll be giving you a sneak peek at these wonderful books in next month's LOVESWEPTs. And immediately following this page, look for a preview of the exciting women's novels from Bantam that are *available now!*

Adam's Fall

Available this month in hardcover
from *New York Times*
bestselling author

SANDRA BROWN

Over the past few years, Lilah Mason had watched her sister Elizabeth find love, get married, and have children, while she's been more than content to channel her energies into a career. A physical therapist with an unsinkable spirit and unwavering compassion, she's one of the best in the field. But when Lilah takes on a demanding new case, her patient's life isn't the only one transformed. She's never had a tougher patient than Adam, who challenges her methods and authority at every turn. Yet Lilah is determined to help him recover the life he's lost. What she can't see is that while she's winning Adam's battle, she's losing her heart. Now, as professional duty and passionate yearnings clash, Lilah must choose the right course for them both.

*Sizzling Romance from One of the
World's Hottest Pens*

Winner of *Romantic Times*'s
1992 Storyteller of the Year Award

Patricia Potter

Nationally bestselling author of
Renegade and **Lightning**

NOTORIOUS

The owner of the most popular saloon in San Francisco, Catalina Hilliard knows Marsh Canton is trouble the moment she first sees him. He's not the first to attempt to open a rival saloon next door to the Silver Slipper, but he does possess a steely strength that was missing from the men she'd driven out of business. Even more perilous to Cat's plans is the spark of desire that flares between them, a desire that's about to spin her carefully orchestrated life out of control . . .

"We have nothing to discuss," she said coldly, even as she struggled to keep from trembling. All her thoughts were in disarray. He was so adept at personal invasion. That look in his eyes of pure radiance, of physical need, almost burned through her.

Fifteen years. Nearly fifteen years since a man had touched her so intimately. And he was doing it only with his eyes!

And, dear Lucifer, she was responding.

She'd thought herself immune from desire. If she'd ever had any, she believed it had been killed long ago by brutality and shame and utter abhorrence of an act that gave men power and left her little more than a thing to be used and hurt. She'd never felt this bubbling, boiling warmth inside, this craving that was more than physical hunger.

That's what frightened her most of all.

But she wouldn't show it. She would never show it! She didn't even like Canton, devil take him. She didn't like anything about him. And she would send him back to wherever he came. Tail between his legs. No matter what it took. And she would never feel desire again.

But now she had little choice, unless she wished to stand here all afternoon, his hand burning a brand into her. He wasn't going to let her go, and perhaps it was time to lay her cards on the table. She preferred open warfare to guerrilla fighting. She hadn't felt right about the kidnapping and beating—even if she did frequently regret her moment of mercy on his behalf.

She shrugged and his hand relaxed slightly. They left, and he flagged down a carriage for hire. Using those strangely elegant manners that still puzzled her, he helped her inside with a grace that would put royalty to shame.

He left her then for a moment and spoke to the driver, passing a few bills up to him, then returned and vaulted to the seat next to her. Hard-muscled thigh pushed against her leg; his tanned arm, made visible by the rolled-up sleeve, touched her much smaller one, the wiry male hair brushing against her skin, sparking a thousand tiny charges. His scent, a spicy mixture of bay and soap, teased her senses. Everything about him—the strength and power and raw masculinity that he made no attempt to conceal—made her feel fragile, delicate.

But not vulnerable, she told herself. Never vulnerable again. She would fight back by seizing control and keeping it.

She straightened her back and smiled. A seductive smile. A smile that had entranced men for the last ten years. A practiced smile that knew exactly how far to go. A kind of promise that left doors opened, while permitting retreat. It was a smile that kept men coming to the Silver Slipper even as they understood they had no real chance of realizing the dream.

Canton raised an eyebrow. "You *are* very good," he said admiringly.

She shrugged. "It usually works."

"I imagine it does," he said. "Although I doubt if most of the men you use it on have seen the thornier part of you."

"Most don't irritate me as you do."

"Irritate, Miss Cat?"

"Don't call me Cat. My name is Catalina."

"Is it?"

"Is yours really Taylor Canton?"

The last two questions were spoken softly, dangerously, both trying to probe weaknesses, and both recognizing the tactic of the other.

"I would swear to it on a Bible," Marsh said, his mouth quirking.

"I'm surprised you have one, or know what one is."

"I had a very good upbringing, Miss Cat." He emphasized the last word.

"And then what happened?" she asked caustically.

The sardonic amusement in his eyes faded. "A great deal. And what is your story?"

Dear God, his voice was mesmerizing, an intimate song that said nothing but wanted everything. Low and deep and provocative. Compelling. And irresistible . . . almost.

"I had a very poor upbringing," she said. "And then a great deal happened."

For the first time since she'd met him, she saw real humor in his eyes. Not just that cynical amusement as if he were some higher being looking down on a world inhabited by silly children. "You're the first woman I've met with fewer scruples than my own," he said, admiration again in his voice.

She opened her eyes wide. "You have some?"

"As I told you that first night, I don't usually mistreat women."

"Usually?"

"Unless provoked."

"A threat, Mr. Canton?"

"I never threaten, Miss Cat. Neither do I turn down challenges."

"And you usually win?"

"Not usually, Miss Cat. Always." The word was flat. Almost ugly in its surety.

"So do I," she said complacently.

Their voices, Cat knew, had lowered into little more than husky whispers. The air in the closed carriage was sparking, hissing, crackling. Threatening to ignite. His hand moved to her arm, his fingers running up and down it in slow, caressingly sensuous trails.

And then the heat surrounding them was as intense as that in the heart of a volcano. Intense and violent. She wondered very briefly if this was a version of hell. She had just decided it was when he bent toward her, his lips brushing over hers.

And heaven and hell collided.

PRINCESS OF THIEVES
by
Katherine O'Neal

"A brilliant new talent bound to
make her mark on the genre."
—Iris Johansen

*Mace Blackwood is the greatest con artist in the world,
a demon whose family is responsible for the death of
Saranda Sherwin's parents. And though he might be
luring her to damnation itself, Saranda allows herself to be set aflame by the fire in his dark eyes. It's a
calculated surrender that he finds both intoxicating
and infuriating, for one evening alone with the
blue-eyed siren can never be enough. And now he
will stop at nothing to have her forever....*

Saranda could read his intentions in the gleam
of his midnight eyes. "Stay away from me," she
gasped.

"Surely, you're not afraid of me? I've already
admitted defeat."

"As if I'd trust anything you'd say."

Mace raised a brow. "Trust? No, sweetheart, it's
not about trust between us."

"You're right. It's about a battle between our
families that has finally come to an end. The

Sherwins have won, Blackwood. You have no further hand to play."

Even as she said it, she knew it wasn't true. Despite the bad blood between them, they had unfinished business. Because the game, this time, had gone too far.

"That's separate. The feud, the competition—that has nothing to do with what's happening between you and me."

"You must think I'm the rankest kind of amateur. Do you think I don't know what you're up to?"

He put his hand to her cheek and stroked the softly shadowed contours of her face. "What am I up to?"

He was so close, she could feel the muscles of his chest toying with her breasts. Against all sense, she hungered to be touched.

"If you can succeed in seducing me, you can run to Winston with the news—"

His hand drifted from her cheek down the naked column of her neck, to softly caress the slope of her naked shoulder. "I could tell him you slept with me whether you do or not. But you know as well as I do he wouldn't believe me."

"That argument won't work either, Blackwood," she said in a dangerously breathy tone.

"Very well, Miss Sherwin. Why don't we just lay our cards on the table?"

"Why not indeed?"

"Then here it is. I don't like you any more than you like me. In fact, I can't think of a woman I'd be less likely to covet. My family cared for yours no more than yours cared for mine. But I find myself in the unfortunate circumstance of wanting you to distraction. For some reason I can't even fathom, I can't look at you without wondering what you'd look like panting in my arms. Without wanting to feel your naked skin beneath my hands. Or taste your sweat on my tongue. Without needing to come inside you and make you cry out in passion and lose some of that *goddamned* control." A faint moan escaped her throat. "You're all I think about. You're like a fever in my brain. I keep thinking if I took you *just once*, I might finally expel you from my mind. So I don't suppose either of us is leaving this office before we've had what you came for."

"I came to tell you—"

"You could have done that any time. You could have left me wondering for the rest of the night if the wedding would take place. But you didn't wait. You knew if this was going to happen, it had to be tonight. Because once you're Winston's wife, I won't come near you. The minute you say 'I do,' you and I take off the gloves, darling, and the real battle begins. So it's now or never." He lowered his mouth to her shoulder, and her breath left her in a sigh.

"Now or never," she repeated in a daze.

"One night to forget who we are and what it all means. You're so confident of winning. Surely, you wouldn't deny me the spoils of the game. Or more to the point . . . deny yourself."

She looked up and met his sweltering gaze. After three days of not seeing him, she'd forgotten how devastatingly handsome he was. "I shan't fall in love with you, if that's what you're thinking. This will give you no advantage over me. I'm still going after you with both barrels loaded."

"Stop trying so hard to figure it out. I don't give a hang what you think of me. And I don't need your tender mercy. I tell you point-blank, if you think you've won, you may be in for a surprise. But that's beside the point." He wrapped a curl around his finger. Then, taking the pins from her hair, one by one, he dropped them to the floor. She felt her taut nerves jump as each pin clicked against the tile.

He ran both hands through the silvery hair, fluffing it with his fingers, dragging them slowly through the length as he watched the play of light on the silky strands. It spilled like moonlight over her shoulders. "Did you have to be so beautiful?" he rasped.

"Do you have to look so much like a Blackwood?"

He looked at her for a moment, his eyes piercing hers, his hands tangled in her hair. "Tell me what you want."

She couldn't look at him. It brought back memories of his brother she'd rather not relive. As it was, she couldn't believe she was doing this. But she had to have him. It was as elemental as food for her body and air to breathe. Her eyes dropped to his mouth—that blatant, sexual mouth that could make her wild with a grin or wet with a word.

She closed her eyes. If she didn't look at him, maybe she could separate this moment from the past. From what his brother had done. Her voice was a mere whisper when she spoke. "I want you to stop wasting time," she told him, "and make love to me."

He let go of her hair and took her naked shoulders in his hands. Bending her backward, he brought his mouth to hers with a kiss so searing, it scalded her heart.

CAPTURE THE NIGHT

by Geralyn Dawson

Award-winning author of

The Texan's Bride

"My highest praise goes to this author
and her work, one of the best . . . I have
read in years."
—*Rendezvous*

*A desperate French beauty, the ruggedly handsome Texan
who rescues her, and their precious stolen "Rose" are swept
together by destiny as they each try to escape the secrets of
their past.*

Madeline groaned as the man called Sinclair sauntered toward her. This is all I need, she thought.

He stopped beside her and dipped into a perfect
imitation of a gentleman's bow. Eyes shining, he
looked up and said in his deplorable French, "Mad-
ame, do you by chance speak English? Apparently,
we'll be sharing a spot in line. I beg to make your
acquaintance."

She didn't answer.

He sighed and straightened. Then a wicked grin creased his face and in English he drawled, "Brazos Sinclair's my name, Texas born and bred. Most of my friends call me Sin, especially my lady friends. Nobody calls me Claire but once. I'll be sailin' with you on the *Uriel*."

Madeline ignored him.

Evidently, that bothered him not at all. "Cute baby," he said, peeking past the blanket. "Best keep him covered good though. This weather'll chill him."

Madeline bristled at the implied criticism. She glared at the man named Sin.

His grin faded. "Sure you don't speak English?"

She held her silence.

"Guess not, huh. That's all right, I'll enjoy conversin' with you anyway." He shot a piercing glare toward Victor Considérant, the colonists' leader and the man who had refused him a place on the *Uriel*. "I need a diversion, you see. Otherwise I'm liable to do something I shouldn't." Angling his head, he gave her another sweeping gaze. "You're a right fine lookin' woman, ma'am, a real beauty. Don't know that I think much of your husband, though, leavin' you here on the docks by your lonesome."

He paused and looked around, his stare snagging on a pair of scruffy sailors. "It's a dangerous thing for women to be alone in such a place, and for a beautiful one like you, well, I hesitate to think."

Obviously, Madeline said to herself.

The Texan continued, glancing around at the people milling along the wharf. " 'Course, I can't say I understand you Europeans. I've been here goin' on two years, and I'm no closer to figurin' y'all out now than I was the day I rolled off the boat." He reached into his jacket pocket and pulled out a pair of peppermint sticks.

Madeline declined the offer by shaking her head, and he returned one to his pocket before taking a slow lick of the second. "One thing, there's all those kings and royals. I think it's nothin' short of silly to climb on a high horse simply because blood family's been plowin' the same dirt for hundreds of years. I tell you what, ma'am, Texans aren't built for bowin'. It's been bred right out of us."

Brazos leveled a hard stare on Victor Considérant and shook his peppermint in the Frenchman's direction. "And aristocrats are just as bad as royalty. That fellow's one of the worst. Although I'll admit that his head's on right about kings and all, his whole notion to create a socialistic city in the heart of Texas is just plain stupid."

Gesturing toward the others who waited ahead of them in line, he said, "Look around you, lady. I'd lay odds not more than a dozen of these folks know the first little bit about farmin', much less what it takes for survivin' on the frontier. Take that crate, for instance." He shook his head incredulously, "They've stored work tools with violins for an ocean crossing, for goodness sake. These folks don't have the sense to pour rain water from a boot!" He popped the candy into his mouth, folded his arms across his chest, and studied the ship, chewing in a pensive silence.

The nerve of the man, Madeline thought, gritting her teeth against the words she'd love to speak. Really, to comment on another's intelligence when his own is so obviously lacking. Listen to his French.

And his powers of observation. Why, she knew how she looked.

Beautiful wasn't the appropriate word.

Brazos swallowed his candy and said, "Hmm. You've given me an idea." Before Madeline gathered her wits to stop him, he leaned over and kissed her cheek. "Thanks, Beauty. And listen, you take care out here without a man to protect you. If I see your husband on this boat I'm goin' to give him a piece of my mind about leavin' you alone." He winked and left her, walking toward the gangway.

Madeline touched the sticky spot on her cheek damp from his peppermint kiss and watched, fascinated despite herself, as the over-bold Texan tapped Considérant on the shoulder. In French that grated on her ears, he said. "Listen Frenchman, I'll make a deal with you. If you find a place for me on your ship I'll be happy to share my extensive knowledge of Texas with any of your folks who'd be interested in learnin'. This land you bought on the Trinity River—it's not more than half a day's ride from my cousin's spread. I've spent a good deal of time in that area over the past few years. I can tell you all about it."

"Mr. Sinclair," Considérant said in English, "please do not further abuse my language. I chose that land myself. Personally. I can answer any questions my peers may have about our new home. Now, as I have told you, this packet has been chartered to sail La Réunion colonists exclusively. Every space is assigned. I sympathize with your need to return to your home, but unfortunately the *Uriel* cannot accommodate you. Please excuse me, Monsieur Sinclair. I have much to see to before we sail. Good day."

"Good day my—" Brazos bit off his words. He turned abruptly and stomped away from the ship. Halting before Madeline, he declared, "This boat ain't leavin' until morning. It's not over yet. By General Taylor's tailor, when it sails, I'm gonna be on it."

He flashed a victorious grin and drawled, "Honey, you've captured my heart and about three other parts. I'll look forward to seein' you aboard ship."

As he walked away, she dropped a handsome gold pocket watch into her reticule, then called out to him in crisp, King's English. "Better you had offered your brain for ballast, Mr. Sinclair. Perhaps then you'd have been allowed aboard the *Uriel*."

And don't miss these spectacular
romances from Bantam Books,
on sale in December

DESIRE
by the nationally bestselling author
Amanda Quick

LONG TIME COMING
a classic romance by the
New York Times
bestselling author
Sandra Brown

STRANGER IN MY ARMS
a thrilling novel of romantic suspense
by **R. J. Kaiser**

WHERE DOLPHINS GO
by bestselling LOVESWEPT author
Peggy Webb
"Ms. Webb has an inventive mind brimming
with originality that makes all of her
books special reading."
—*Romantic Times*

And in hardcover from Doubleday

AMAZON LILY
by *Theresa Weir*
"Romantic adventure has no finer writer than
the spectacular Theresa Weir."
—*Romantic Times*

OFFICIAL RULES

To enter the sweepstakes below carefully follow all instructions found elsewhere in this offer.

The **Winners Classic** will award prizes with the following approximate maximum values: 1 Grand Prize: $26,500 (or $25,000 cash alternate); 1 First Prize: $3,000; 5 Second Prizes: $400 each; 35 Third Prizes: $100 each; 1,000 Fourth Prizes: $7.50 each. Total maximum retail value of Winners Classic Sweepstakes is $42,500. Some presentations of this sweepstakes may contain individual entry numbers corresponding to one or more of the aforementioned prize levels. To determine the Winners, individual entry numbers will first be compared with the winning numbers preselected by computer. For winning numbers not returned, prizes will be awarded in random drawings from among all eligible entries received. Prize choices may be offered at various levels. If a winner chooses an automobile prize, all license and registration fees, taxes, destination charges and, other expenses not offered herein are the responsibility of the winner. If a winner chooses a trip, travel must be complete within one year from the time the prize is awarded. Minors must be accompanied by an adult. Travel companion(s) must also sign release of liability. Trips are subject to space and departure availability. Certain black-out dates may apply.

The following applies to the sweepstakes named above:

No purchase necessary. You can also enter the sweepstakes by sending your name and address to: P.O. Box 508, Gibbstown, N.J. 08027. Mail each entry separately. Sweepstakes begins 6/1/93. Entries must be received by 12/30/94. Not responsible for lost, late, damaged, misdirected, illegible or postage due mail. Mechanically reproduced entries are not eligible. All entries become property of the sponsor and will not be returned.

Prize Selection/Validations: Selection of winners will be conducted no later than 5:00 PM on January 28, 1995, by an independent judging organization whose decisions are final. Random drawings will be held at 1211 Avenue of the Americas, New York, N.Y. 10036. Entrants need not be present to win. Odds of winning are determined by total number of entries received. Circulation of this sweepstakes is estimated not to exceed 200 million. All prizes are guaranteed to be awarded and delivered to winners. Winners will be notified by mail and may be required to complete an affidavit of eligibility and release of liability which must be returned within 14 days of date on notification or alternate winners will be selected in a random drawing. Any prize notification letter or any prize returned to a participating sponsor, Bantam Doubleday Dell Publishing Group, Inc., its participating divisions or subsidiaries, or the independent judging organization as undeliverable will be awarded to an alternate winner. Prizes are not transferable. No substitution for prizes except as offered or as may be necessary due to unavailability, in which case a prize of equal or greater value will be awarded. Prizes will be awarded approximately 90 days after the drawing. All taxes are the sole responsibility of the winners. Entry constitutes permission (except where prohibited by law) to use winners' names, hometowns, and likenesses for publicity purposes without further or other compensation. Prizes won by minors will be awarded in the name of parent or legal guardian.

Participation: Sweepstakes open to residents of the United States and Canada, except for the province of Quebec. Sweepstakes sponsored by Bantam Doubleday Dell Publishing Group, Inc., (BDD), 1540 Broadway, New York, NY 10036. Versions of this sweepstakes with different graphics and prize choices will be offered in conjunction with various solicitations or promotions by different subsidiaries and divisions of BDD. Where applicable, winners will have their choice of any prize offered at level won. Employees of BDD, its divisions, subsidiaries, advertising agencies, independent judging organization, and their immediate family members are not eligible.

Canadian residents, in order to win, must first correctly answer a time limited arithmetical skill testing question. Void in Puerto Rico, Quebec and wherever prohibited or restricted by law. Subject to all federal, state, local and provincial laws and regulations. For a list of major prize winners (available after 1/29/95) send a self-addressed, stamped envelope entirely separate from your entry to: Sweepstakes Winners, P.O. Box 517, Gibbstown, NJ 08027. Requests must be received by 12/30/94. DO NOT SEND ANY OTHER CORRESPONDENCE TO THIS P.O. BOX.

Don't miss these fabulous Bantam women's fiction titles

now on sale

• NOTORIOUS
by Patricia Potter, author of *RENEGADE*

Long ago, Catalina Hilliard had vowed never to give away her heart, but she hadn't counted on the spark of desire that flared between her and her business rival, Marsh Canton. Now that desire is about to spin Cat's carefully orchestrated life out of control.

_____56225-8 $5.50/6.50 in Canada

• PRINCESS OF THIEVES
by Katherine O'Neal, author of *THE LAST HIGHWAYMAN*

Mace Blackwood was a daring rogue—the greatest con artist in the world. Saranda Sherwin was a master thief who used her wits and wiles to make tough men weak. And when Saranda's latest charade leads to tragedy and sends her fleeing for her life, Mace is compelled to follow, no matter what the cost.

_____56066-2 $5.50/$6.50 in Canada

• CAPTURE THE NIGHT
by Geralyn Dawson

In this "Once Upon a Time" Romance with "Beauty and the Beast" at its heart, Geralyn Dawson weaves the love story of a runaway beauty, the Texan who rescues her, and their precious stolen "Rose."

_____56176-6 $4.99/5.99 in Canada